THE TREASURE IN THE LITTLE TRUNK

THE TREASURE IN THE LITTLE TRUNK

BY
HELEN FULLER ORTON

WITH EMBELLISHMENTS BY
ROBERT BALL

J. B. LIPPINCOTT COMPANY
PHILADELPHIA   NEW YORK

1369

5/5/69

THIRTIETH PRINTING

Library of Congress Catalog Card Number 32-22715

Printed in the United States of America

CONTENTS

[v]

CONTENTS

THE TREASURE IN THE LITTLE TRUNK

CHAPTER I

PATTY'S SAMPLER

IT was a cold afternoon in the late winter of the year 1823. In a little Vermont village, school was out and the boys and girls had scampered out of the schoolhouse with whoops of joy.

Patty Armstrong and Jane Marvin were going home together, swinging their dinner pails as they walked. The snow crunched under their feet at each step and lay in deep drifts along the fences at the side. They were both nine "going on ten," as Patty always said when asked her age. Almost every day since they began going to school they had taken this walk together morning and afternoon.

Sometimes Kanah Armstrong, Patty's brother, walked with them, but this day he had stayed behind to have a snow fight with some of the boys. The girls were suddenly aware that he

[1]

was coming when a snowball hit Patty's blue hood.

"Kanah Armstrong!" she shouted. "I'll give you a good one."

She stooped and quickly scooped up snow for a snowball, but before she had time to throw it, another one came, hitting Jane's red hood. Then began a battle of snowballs. The two girls could make them faster than Kanah could alone, so they soon had the best of it, although he was two years older.

"I'll quit if you will," he said, finally.

But instead of waiting to walk with them, he ran ahead and was soon out of sight around a bend in the road. As the two girls arrived at the gate, he could be seen going off through the orchard with his sled.

"Come on home with me for a little while," begged Jane, who lived a quarter of a mile farther on.

"I can't to-day, Jane. I have to go in and work on my sampler," Patty replied.

"Oh, bother! Always working on that sampler," pouted Jane.

"But I have only a week to finish it, you know," said Patty. "I won't get the string of gold beads unless I finish it by the time I am ten."

"Well, then, I'll go home and piece blocks,"

[2]

said Jane, "but I'd rather stay out and slide down hill, wouldn't you?"

"Of course," admitted Patty. "Who wouldn't?"

That evening, after supper, a fire was blazing

The Fireside

merrily in the huge fireplace in the kitchen of the Armstrong home. The flames lit up that part of the room, but all the rest of it was in shadow. They warmed that part of the room, but all the rest was cold.

On a low stool in front of the fireplace Patty

[3]

sat working on her sampler. It was a square piece of coarse cloth on which she was making with careful stitches the letters of the alphabet. In fact, she was making five alphabets on it, each one in a different pattern, so that she would have a sample to copy from when she wished to put an initial on anything. In addition to the alphabets, she was to work a border of flowers and trees and other pretty designs; and at the bottom of it she was to place a verse. By the light of the dancing flames, she was now pushing her needle in and out, making a capital T with blue silk thread.

"Oh, dear! There are such a lot of stitches on a sampler," she sighed.

Grandmother was sitting on the settle, which stood at one side of the fireplace, knitting a woolen sock for Kanah. His real name was Elkanah, but seldom did any one take the trouble to say all of it. Grandmother was so deft at knitting that she did not have to look at her work, so the dancing light of the flames did not bother her, but Patty was bending over to count the threads of the cloth, for she must take only so many threads up for each stitch.

Father came in from the barn, where he had just finished doing the evening chores.

"Aren't there any candles?" he asked.

"Only a very few left," said Mother. "I am

saving those to use if company comes, or if we want a light after the fire is banked at night. We have had so many dark days this winter that the candles I made in the fall haven't lasted as they usually do."

"Have we any tallow for making new candles?" he asked.

"Yes," Mother replied. "I am going to make some to-morrow."

"Oh, Mother, may I stay home from school and help you?" begged Patty.

"If you stay at home from school, you had better work on your sampler," said Grandmother. "You remember that it has to be done before you are ten years old."

Patty sighed as she attempted to get a knot out of the worsted with which she was working the T. A long task had it been for a lively girl of nine who had often had to sit and work letters when she was wanting to go outdoors and play.

"I remember," she replied to Grandmother's remark, "and I do want that string of gold beads. I want it more than anything else in the world."

"Oh, Patty, don't set your heart on a bauble of that sort. It will perhaps make you proud, every time you wear it," cautioned Mother. "For my part, I think it just as well that you

[5]

should not have the string of beads till you are much older."

Father looked up from the book he was reading. "Patience will not let a piece of jewelry turn her head and make her proud," he said. "I am sure she has more sense than that, even if she is only nine."

"Most likely Patty will lose them before she has had them a month," spoke up Kanah, who was at the other side of the fireplace, whittling an arrow with his jackknife.

"I won't lose them," protested Patty. "I will not part with them as long as I live. I will be as careful as can be, every time I wear them, and I will keep them safe in their box when I am not wearing them. So there!"

"Oh, I don't think she will lose them," said Mother, "and I hope they won't spoil her."

"We must remember that it is according to the will," said Grandmother. "The eldest girl in each generation is to have the beads by the time she is ten, if she has finished her first sampler neatly. I think we can trust Patty to do the right thing."

Father got up to put some more wood on the fire. As he poked the half-burned logs, the sparks flew up the great chimney and soon the flames burst merrily forth. They lighted the far corners of the room. They made the pewter dishes sparkle in the dancing firelight. They showed the strings of dried apples and hops and onions and the ears of popcorn hanging from the rafters. They revealed the spinning-wheel in the far corner and the long table on which the family ate their meals.

In the fireplace itself, from a swinging bar of iron, called a crane, there hung a teakettle and another kettle, both of iron. Near by, against the bricks, there hung a fire-shovel and a warming-pan. A pair of tongs for handling the wood stood at one side. At the other side, built into the wall, was the brick oven in which Mrs. Armstrong did her baking. A cozy place it was, on this cold winter evening, with the blazing fire roaring up the chimney.

Mother brought some candle-wicking and began to cut it into lengths to make candles about ten inches long. This she could do in the evening and thus save time in the day.

"May I help you dip candles?" asked Patty again.

"Why, Patty, it is time you were learning how to do it, but you must work on your sampler, you know."

"But if I promise to finish this in the afternoon, then may I help you in the morning?" pleaded Patty.

"You had better let her help," said Father.

[7]

"Samplers are all right and of course Patty has to finish hers soon; but she has to learn to do many useful things and she might as well start on candle making."

"I'll be glad to have some one help me," said Mother. "Now, when I was younger than Patty, I had made two samplers and had learned to—"

She was interrupted by a knock on the kitchen door. Kanah sprang to open it, but the visitor had already lifted the latch and opened the door.

"Why, Tom Marvin!" exclaimed Kanah, in surprise. "Where did you come from?"

"How do you do, Tom?" said Mother. "We are glad to see you."

"We thought you were still out west—had no idea you were back in this country," said Father, as he shook hands with Jane's brother.

"I came home to get my wife and the baby," he said. "I have cleared some land and built a log house and everything is ready for them."

He went over to shake hands with Grandmother.

"It seems good to see you folks," he continued. "That is the only trouble with the country where I have been. One doesn't see many folks out there."

"What sort of country is it?" asked Kanah.

"Do you like it there?" asked Mother.

"Are all the things we hear about its being such a grand country true?" asked Mr. Armstrong, as he took his seat by the fireplace once more.

"Do I like it?" said Tom. "Why, the land is so rich that corn will grow as high as this room. And you should just see the great yellow pumpkins and potatoes and squashes that grow there."

"But aren't there lots of trees?" asked Kanah, standing with his arms over Tom's chair.

Tom laughed. "Trees? Why, there is nothing but trees for miles and miles, except now and then a clearing, where a settler has chopped them down, or one the Indians have made."

"It must be a sight of work to chop down hundreds of trees," said Mother.

"It is work, to be sure," Tom replied, "but who cares about hard work?"

"Just where is this place you have settled in?" asked Grandmother.

"Away over in the western part of New York State," replied Tom. "That is what it is called —Western New York. If you go down to Albany and then west about three hundred miles, along the Mohawk River and beyond—why, there you are."

"I must say that I think this place is good enough," said Mother. "I can't see why any-

[9]

body wants to go away from good old Vermont. I like its mountains."

"Oh, Vermont is all right. I like it, too. But you know what a lot of stones are on the land around here. Now, on the land I have bought, you can hardly find a stone to throw at a cat."

"Why should you want to throw stones at a cat?" asked Patty, wide-eyed. "Don't you like cats?"

Tom laughed. "I don't like wildcats," he replied, "and it was a wildcat that came toward me one day when I was off in the woods without a gun."

At this, Kanah came closer. "A wildcat! And have you ever seen a bear there?"

"A bear? I've seen several bears. And wolves! You should hear them howl these cold winter nights."

"Well, all I can say is, I am glad we live in a part of the country that is settled and where there aren't wild animals," said Mother.

Father, however, was eager to put more questions about this new country.

"I have often thought I would like to move out there," he said. "I work hard all the summer long on this farm and have very poor crops. I am getting tired of it. And then the taxes are so high that we can hardly make both ends meet."

[10]

"There are lots of folks going there this year from all over New England," said Tom. "On the way back here I met dozens of loaded sleighs. I wouldn't come back here to live, not if you would give me this whole county free."

"Well, I want to know," said Mr. Armstrong.

They talked for an hour about the new land and other things. They talked about Patty's sampler and her string of beads. Then Tom said, "I'll have to be going."

"Come again to see us," urged Mother.

"Thank you. I'll come if I can possibly find time."

Then, as he started for the door, he said to Patty, "I wish you good luck with your sampler and your beads."

All this time Patty's little sister, Mary Ann, was asleep in her trundle-bed in the big bedroom that opened off the kitchen. Soon the tall clock in the front room showed the hour of nine. Grandmother put aside her knitting and Mother finished cutting the candle-wicks. Patty folded up her sampler and put it and the pretty yarns away.

Mother took the warming-pan from its peg beside the fireplace and filled it with hot embers. It was a round brass pan, with a very long handle and a cover perforated with little holes. She carried it by the long handle first to Grandmother's bedroom, where she moved it quickly back and forth between the sheets, to warm the bed on this cold night. Then she went to each bed in the house and did the same thing. Well it was that she did this, for without it the sheets were as cold as the snow that lay outside like a white blanket over all the earth.

Mr. Armstrong fixed the fire for the night. He raked the embers together into a heap and covered them with ashes. "Banking the fire," he called it. He did it so the fire would keep all night. If it should go out, there were no matches with which to start another one, for matches were not yet known. He might light it with flint and tinder, but it was a hard task to do that, because sometimes it was almost impossible to make the kindling catch fire.

Finally they were all asleep. The house was quiet inside, but outside the wind howled around the corners and whistled around the chimney; and the tall evergreens moaned in the wind.

CHAPTER II

BORROWING FIRE

THE next morning, before it was light, Mr. Armstrong got up and went into the kitchen to unbank the fire and put fresh wood on it, so as to have it going well by the time the others were up. He uncovered the fire —raked the ashes from the coals he had buried the night before—but not a live coal could he find.

"I hope the fire hasn't gone out," he thought.

By poking around among the ashes, he found a few burnt embers that had a little warmth in them.

"Perhaps if I use the bellows, they will start up," he said aloud.

He took the bellows that hung beside the fireplace and blew on the embers, but not a spark of fire appeared.

"There is nothing to do but try to strike fire with the flint," he thought. "I hope it won't take long this cold morning."

At the side of the fireplace there hung a little round tin box in which were a piece of steel and a flint and some old pieces of scorched linen. He struck the steel against the flint to make a spark with which he hoped to set the linen on fire. "Tinder," he called it. If he succeeded, he could then light the kindling-wood with that. Several times a spark flew off as he struck the flint and steel together, but each time it went out before the tinder was set on fire.

"I can't waste time this way," he said to himself, after fifteen minutes had passed. "Kanah will have to go and borrow some fire."

He went to the foot of the stairs that led to the attic bedroom.

"Kanah! Kanah!" he called. "Get up and run to Neighbor Marvin's for some fire. Ours has gone out."

Kanah opened his eyes, and shivered as he thought of the cold run through the snow on this wintry morning.

"Can't you start it with the flint?" he asked.

"No, it won't catch this morning," replied Father. "I have been trying for fifteen minutes and I can't waste any more time. Hurry up!"

Kanah was eleven, going on twelve, big enough to do a great many things. Sometimes he wished he wasn't so big. It wasn't fair, hav· ing to be the one to go on all the hard errands. Patty never had to go out into the cold and take that long walk through the snow in zero weather for fire. In spite of his grumbling he got up and quickly pulled on his clothes of heavy homespun and ran downstairs.

"The wind blew so hard last night that it must have drawn too much and made the fire burn out," said Father. "Take the warming-pan to carry it in. And be quick, for it is terribly cold here this morning."

Kanah put on his heavy coat, his fur cap and the warm mittens that Grandmother had knitted for him and started off toward the Marvin house with the warming-pan in his hand. He went across lots, through the orchard and the fields. The snow was so hard that it would bear his weight in most places.

When he had knocked on the side door and Mrs. Marvin had opened it, she said, "Good morning, Kanah. I can guess why you have come so early in the morning. Your fire is out."

"You guessed right," he replied. "Have you folks any to spare?"

"Yes; we have a pretty good fire this morning," she said. "Let me take the warming-pan."

The fireplace was full of blazing wood and a kettle was singing over the flames, as it hung by a chain from a bar in the top of the fireplace. Mrs. Marvin took the fire-shovel, scooped up some red-hot coals and placed them in the warming-pan.

[15]

"Thank you," said Kanah. "I'll hurry home. Our house is as cold as all outdoors this morning."

"Good luck to you in getting them safe there," said Mrs. Marvin.

But luck was not with him, for about half way home he slipped on a piece of icy snow and went sprawling on the ground. The cover of the warming-pan came loose and the precious fire went flying in all directions over the snow, making sizzling sounds as it struck.

"Oh, botheration!" he said, as he ruefully looked at the empty pan.

He started back to the Marvin house. "Maybe she won't want to give me any more," he was thinking, as he waited for the door to be opened.

"Well, well, Kanah! That was bad luck," she said, smiling. "You'll have to try again."

She took the fire-shovel and once more scooped up some glowing pieces of wood and placed them in the pan. This time he got them safely home.

Mother was up now and had just come into the kitchen saying, "Mercy me! Is the fire out?"

He helped Mother build it. Soon the flames were roaring up the chimney, the kettle of corn mush was simmering on the crane, the coffee was boiling, and the griddle for the buckwheat pancakes was hanging from a chain, ready to bake the pancakes for breakfast.

"Wouldn't it be fine if there was some easier way of making fire than with flint and steel?" said Father, at breakfast.

"And easier than going for fire through the snow on a bitter cold morning," added Kanah.

"Maybe there will be, sometime," said Father. "I have often thought it might be done. Why couldn't there be a little stick with something on the end of it to strike fire?"

"That would be nice," said Mother.

"You mark my word, some one will think of a way to do it sometime," declared Father.

CHAPTER III

CANDLE-MAKING

AFTER breakfast Mother said, "You may work on your sampler an hour or two, Patty, while I make the pies and put them in the oven to bake."

Taking her sampler, her needle and the pretty silks, Patty sat down by the window, where she could get a good light this dull morning. Though she had finished the five alphabets, there was still the verse to be worked at the bottom. These are the words that Patty began to work on the coarse cloth:

Patty Armstrong is my name,
Nine years old I did the same.
When I am gone and this you see,
Then keep it to remember me.

When Mother had finished rolling out the pie crusts and had put them in the pie pans, with mincemeat between the crusts, she went to the oven at the side of the fireplace, where she opened the iron door. Inside the oven, where

[18]

wood had been burning for a long time, there was now a mass of embers, red-hot.

She pulled out the embers with shovel and poker and brushed the last ashes out with a turkey wing. She closed the draft at the top of the oven and put the pies and some loaves of bread and a pot of beans in to bake. Then she closed the door.

"There! That is done. And now you and I will go at the candle-making," she said to Patty.

Mother already had two large iron kettles of tallow heating over the fire. She now went to the attic and brought down a number of small round sticks about fifteen inches long. From each stick she hung seven of the wicks she had cut the night before.

"See, Patty, this is the way to do it," she said, as Patty tried in vain to get the wicks to hang straight. "Pull them down gently, over and over between your fingers."

Patty did as she was told and then soon her stick of wicks was ready to be dipped into the tallow in one of the big kettles.

Mother now took two long poles and placed them across two chairs, so that they looked like the sides of a ladder without any rounds. Father lifted one of the big kettles from the fire and placed it on the floor, where it could be easily reached.

Mother took one of the small sticks and dipped the whole seven wicks in the fat at once. Then she laid it across the long sticks that were resting on the two chairs. It looked like the round of a ladder. Patty tried to dip her wicks, but she found it harder than she had thought. Mother showed her again how to do it.

Then she dipped hers and hung it over the two long poles, next to Mother's. The fat on the wicks soon hardened.

"Oh, but what tiny candles they are!" said Patty in a disappointed tone. "I thought they were going to be nice big candles like our others."

"Just wait," said Mother. "Watch and see what will happen."

They dipped the wicks till all the hundred candles had been dipped once.

"Now we'll start over," said Mother. "We'll dip them all again."

She took the first ones and dipped them again. By this time the first kettle had been put back and the other kettle was on the floor. Patty dipped her first row of candles a second time. When they had cooled, she said, "Oh, see how much mine have grown!"

Indeed they were much bigger around. She

and Mother kept dipping them over and over till they were big enough.

There the hundred candles were hanging in rows.

"What a pretty sight they are, Mother!" said Patty.

"You may fill the candle-box," said Mother.

Patty was just stretching up to take down the candle-box that hung by the fireplace, when there was a knock on the door. Before they could get there to open it, in came a lady wrapped up in so many shawls and cloaks that one could hardly tell whether she was a young person or an old one, a stout one or a thin one. But in a moment, Patty exclaimed, "Why, good morning, Aunt Polly!"

"I am so glad to see you, sister Polly," said Mother. "It has been so stormy lately that I declare we haven't seen any one for a week, except Tom Marvin."

"So you have seen Tom, too, have you?" asked Aunt Polly. "He seems to think it is a grand country out there in the west. Did he tell you how much he likes it?"

"Yes, he did. I began to be afraid he would persuade Daniel to sell out and go there."

Uncle Reuben Foster, who had stayed outside to put a blanket on the horse and to tie him to the hitching-post and to see that all was right in the cutter, now came in, just in time to hear the last words.

"Where is it that Daniel Armstrong is going if he sells out?" he asked.

"Out west, where Tom Marvin is going to live," Mother answered.

"It wouldn't be a bad idea," said Uncle Reuben. "It must be a mighty fine country. Maybe we'll all be going before another year."

"Why, Reuben Foster! Indeed, we won't," declared Aunt Polly. "We won't leave our home and our friends to go off to a wilderness to live."

All this time Patty had been busy filling the candle-box with some of the new candles. She had hung it once more on the wall near the fireplace.

"What a nice lot of candles you have made," said Aunt Polly. "But why isn't Patty in school to-day?"

"I stayed at home to work on my sampler," Patty spoke up. "And to help Mother with the candle-making," she added proudly.

"Well, as to the sampler, I think getting your lessons is more important than doing fancy-work," said Aunt Polly.

"But Patty has to have it done by her birth-day next week," said Grandmother Armstrong. "You know about the string of beads, don't you?"

"Oh, yes, to be sure," admitted Aunt Polly, "but if she were my girl, she wouldn't wear such expensive jewelry when she is so young."

Uncle Reuben now went over to the fireplace and put some more wood on the fire.

"In this weather the fireplaces burn up heaps of wood," he remarked, "and even then one can't keep warm more than half way across the room."

"The water is frozen an inch thick on that bucket of water over there in this very room," said Aunt Polly.

"I know it," Mother answered, "and we have one of the warmest houses around here, too. Fireplaces are pretty to look at, but wouldn't it be nice if there were some way to distribute the heat through the room, instead of making us roast in one part of it and freeze in the other?"

"Maybe some one will think up a way to do it sometime," said Uncle Reuben. "I shouldn't wonder at all if it could be done."

"What do people ever do who live in log houses, as they used to?" said Mother.

"And the way a lot of folks live now, on the back roads," said Grandmother.

"And the way they all live in that new country out west, where these men-folks want to go?" said Aunt Polly.

"I am glad we have this nice house," said **Patty.**

[23]

"Nice house," echoed little Mary Ann.

Indeed it was a nice house, not a great mansion, but pleasant and comfortable; and some parts of it were beautiful.

The front room, which they used only when company came, had a fireplace as big as the one in the kitchen. A tall clock stood in one corner. There was a highboy of cherry wood on one side and a beautiful carved chest, called a Hadley chest—one of Mother's wedding gifts—on the other side. There were lovely, graceful chairs. On some shelves in one corner, there were a number of books, and some shells, beautiful sea-shells, which great-great-grandfather had brought home on one of his voyages. Patty thought there never could be a prettier room.

It was a good-looking house on the outside, too; it was painted white and stood in a sightly location, where the family could look off over the valleys and fields to the mountains. The whole place was most conveniently arranged, for all the buildings were connected. Father could go from the kitchen to the woodshed, then through the tool-house and from that to the barn to feed the stock on cold winter mornings, without once going outside in the cold.

The prettiest thing of all was the front door. It was paneled, with glass at the sides, and over the top a fanlight, a beautiful arrangement of panes of glass, spreading out like a fan. Patty was rather proud of their house. Mother felt a great contentment with it.

When Aunt Polly and Uncle Reuben had gone, Mother said, "It worries me a bit that all these men are becoming discontented with things here. I can't blame Daniel much for wanting a change, he works so hard and gets so little for it. But it would be many a long day before we would have as good a place to live in as this."

CHAPTER IV

THE GOLD BEADS

A WEEK later the weather had turned warmer and the melting snow from the roof was dripping from the eaves. It was evening. There was a blazing fire in the fireplace of the front room, and mysterious whisperings had been going on ever since Patty and Kanah came home from school, for this was Patty's birthday.

The sampler was finished and had been pronounced very well done by Grandmother and Mother. It was now fastened up on the wall, where every one could see it.

Grandmother was wearing her very best dress of black silk and her cap of lace and mull. Mother had on her second-best dress, for she did not want to take the chance of spoiling her very best one with the refreshments she was going to serve later.

Patty herself had on her blue merino, trimmed with rows of narrow black velvet ribbon.

"We'll have a little celebration," Mother had said at supper time. "A girl is ten years old but once. I have invited the Marvins over."

A little later they came, Mr. and Mrs. Marvin, Tom Marvin and his wife, Melia, and their baby, and, of course, Patty's best friend, Jane.

Each one of the Marvins brought a gift for Patty. Kanah gave her the bow and arrows he had been making with his jackknife.

"Don't s'pose you can shoot it far," he said. "But I know you've been wanting one."

Mother gave her the cloth for a new dress, which she had woven herself, and Father gave her a book called *The History of the Fairchild Family,* that he had brought home the last time he had gone to market in the town twenty miles away.

The crowning gift was the one Grandmother was holding in her hand. When it came her turn, she said, "This gift that I have been keeping for Patty has come down from long ago. My grandmother, Patty's great-great-grandmother, had it first. It was given to her when she was ten years old for an act of bravery."

Patty had heard the story many times, but she now listened eagerly, as did all the rest, while Grandmother went on: "Once upon a time, a

long, long time ago, there was a little girl and
her name was Patty. Her whole name was Patience Marilla Allen. Her father was a sea-cap-
tain and was away on a voyage.

"Patience was often put in charge of her lit-

The Birthday Party

tle sister, when they went out to play. One day,
when they were in the yard, the little sister fell
into the well. Quick as a wink Patty threw herself on her stomach and reached down into the
water. In a moment the curly head of the sister
came to the surface and she grasped it by the
hair and held it above the water.

[28]

"She could not possibly lift the little sister out alone, nor could she long keep from slipping in herself if she kept holding on, but she called over her shoulder to her small brother, 'Run to the house and tell Mother to come quick.'

"It took several minutes for the little boy to run to the house and the mother to run down there. Patty's fingers became numb and she could scarcely hold on. Finally the little sister began to slip from her grasp, but she held on with all her might till her mother came. When her father came home, not long afterward, he brought many lovely things, but the most beautiful was a string of gold beads. He gave them to his little daughter and had her initials put on the clasp—P. M. A."

"They are just the same as Patty's," said Jane.

"Yes, just the same," said Grandmother. "Well, that first Patty got them because she did a brave and beautiful deed; but she knew that not every girl has an opportunity to do something brave, so in her will she said that in each generation they should go to the eldest girl if she finished a sampler by the time she was ten— and did it neatly. So now they are Patty's beads."

Grandmother handed Patty the box with the precious beads in. It was a box of smooth, beautiful wood, lined with rich red velvet. Mother fastened the beads on her neck. Very lovely they looked against the blue merino dress.

"Patty will lose them before she has them very long," said Kanah.

"No, I won't," declared Patty. "I'll keep them always. I'll never, never part with them."

"It must be wonderful to have something that is so old and has such a story as they have," said Jane.

For an hour there were games and fun. Then Mother and Kanah brought in hot maple syrup and a pewter platter of doughnuts and another of light biscuit, which Mother had just taken from the oven—delicious eatables for a birthday party in Vermont in that year 1823.

Now that the party was nearly at an end, Tom and Melia Marvin said they must be going, for there were many last things to do before they started west the next morning.

"We are all wishing you the very best of luck in the new land," said Mr. Armstrong.

After they had left, Mother said, "What a delicate thing Melia Marvin is! To think of her going out to a rough, unsettled country to live in a log cabin!"

"She is young and wiry," said Grandmother. "She'll make out."

"I wish I could go," said Jane. "I think it

would be fun to go away off and see things. Don't you, Patty?"

"Yes, I would like to," said Patty.

She was to have that wish granted sooner than she thought.

CHAPTER V

PACKING TO GO

IT was only a few days later when Patty and Kanah realized that Father and Mother were anxious over something. They were frequently talking about a note that Father had signed with a cousin.

"You see, I promised to pay that note if he couldn't," said Father, "and I am afraid I will have to do it."

"But how can we?" asked Mother. "Where will we get the money?"

"We may have to sell the farm," said Father, with sadness in his voice.

"Sell the farm? Sell this nice house where we have lived so long?" said Mother.

"We might," said Father.

It soon proved to be true. When they found out that it really had to be done, though, it was quite astonishing how brave Mother was about it. When Kanah and Patty were told, she said, "Now don't you two make a lot of fuss about it, for Father feels sorry enough as it is. We'll all just have to make the best of it."

"There will be a little money left," said Father. "We can start over again. We might go to that new country where Tom Marvin has gone."

"Yes, that is the very best thing to do," agreed Mother.

Father was surprised at this, knowing how much she liked their house, but pleased, too, for it was the very thing he had been wishing all winter to do.

Patty said to Jane, as they walked to school through the melting snow, "What do you think we are going to do? Move away from here. Going out west."

"Why, Patty Armstrong! I didn't think you would ever go off and leave me. What shall I do without you?"

"Well, we have to go," said Patty. "I don't understand all about it, but Father and Mother think it is best."

"When are you going?" asked Jane, almost in tears.

"Just as soon as we can get ready," Patty replied.

"Oh, but I'll miss you," said Jane. "Here we have walked to school together every morning all these years."

"And I'll miss you, Jane. I'll miss you more than tongue can tell, but my folks are going,

[33]

so there is nothing to do but go along." Then she added, "Won't it be grand, though, to take a long journey and see things?"

Before very long Father had found some one to buy the place. Then he went to an agent of the Holland Land Company, which owned a large part of Western New York, and signed a contract to buy a farm in the Genesee country. Next he had a white canvas cover put on their lumber wagon.

"That wagon won't hold nearly all the furniture and things we'd like to take," said Mother.

"No, that is true," said Father. "We'll have to choose the most necessary things and leave the rest."

When Aunt Polly learned what they were planning to do, she said, "I wouldn't go to that new country to live, even if it were given to me. Nothing but woods and mosquitoes and swamps and log houses—and wild animals. And there won't be any church or school."

"You'll see how fast I'll chop down the trees on our land and make a clearing and build a log house and plant some crops," said Father. "After a few years, we'll have fences and a garden and a fine house."

Choosing the things to take was a difficult task. Of course they must take an axe for chopping down trees and a pickaxe and a crowbar for digging up roots and a plow for plowing the land when it was cleared. They must have a shovel and a hoe and a big log-chain. They must have a hammer and a saw, some augers and a chisel.

"We must take the churn and the spinning-wheel along," said Mother, "and of course the bedquilts and the feather beds and the pillows must go. We can't get along without a long-handled frying-pan and two kettles, a small one for cooking food and a large one for making soap, and we must have a tea kettle, a pancake griddle and some jugs for water."

"Can my sled go?" asked Kanah.

"No; I can make you another one next fall," said Father. "We'll have to have room for some bags of wheat for flour and for seed; and we'll need some corn for meal and for seed."

The pewter dishes Mother managed to tuck in here and there—the plates and the mugs and the two big platters and the children's porrin-gers—but the china ones would surely get broken, so she left them with Aunt Polly.

Well, after they had packed in food for the journey and a chair and the little leather trunk with their best clothes in, there didn't seem to be much room left.

"Aren't we going to take the beds?' asked Patty.

[35]

"Can't manage," Father replied. "I can build some beds there."

"I do wish I could take my carved chest," said Mother.

"So do I," said Father, "but how can we get such a big thing in, with all the other things we must carry? That and the highboy can't be managed. I'll make you a chest after a time. It won't be carved as beautifully as this, but it will be as large."

The shelves in the corner needn't be taken, but Patty took the pretty sea-shells and put them in the little leather trunk.

"We must have some books," said Mother. "We must have a Bible and some schoolbooks and a few of the others." So she found a place for them.

Aunt Polly offered to keep the rest of the books, the beautiful chest, the tall clock, the highboy and the lovely chairs.

"Maybe there will be a way to get them to you sometime," she said.

The day before they started, Mother went to the yard and began to dig here and there.

"What are you doing that for?" asked Patty.

"I'm going to take these tulip and hyacinth and daffodil bulbs with me," said Mother. "I'm going to take some slips from my roses, too, and some roots from the lilac bushes."

"Why do you do that?" asked Patty. "Won't there be any flowers in those woods?"

"Yes, there will be plenty of wild flowers, but it will seem more like home if I have my favorite flowers in that strange place."

She put them all in a bag and found a place for them in the wagon.

"Where shall we pack the string of beads?" asked Patty. "They are my greatest treasure."

"They had better be carried in the little trunk," said Mother. "That is the safest place for them, among the best clothes."

"I don't see how we are all going to ride," said Patty. "There is only one seat and that will hold only three."

"Well, Mother and Mary Ann will sit on the seat," said Father. "I'll sit there part of the time. You can have a turn there sometimes. I expect that Kanah and I will walk a good share of the way. You and Kanah won't mind perching on some of the bags or bundles, will you?"

"I think that will be fun," said Patty.

Ever since they had begun to pack, Grandmother had been looking on with a heavy heart. "I have half a mind to go along," she said. "I'll miss you folks a heap."

"We'd like to have you go with us," said Father, "but this is going to be no easy journey and we wouldn't want you to get sick. After a while we'll have a more comfortable house than a log cabin; and maybe there will be some easier way to go."

"Maybe I'll surprise you sometime," she said.

So she went to live with another son, a few miles away. Aunt Polly and Uncle Reuben came to see them off. Mr. and Mrs. Marvin and Jane came. Aunt Polly, although she did not approve of their going, brought along some presents—a large bag of ginger cookies and some strings of dried apples and a crock of apple butter for them to eat on the way. Mrs. Marvin gave Mother a log-cabin quilt and a batch of doughnuts and six loaves of bread baked in her brick oven just the night before.

"I am dreadfully sorry you are going away," she said. "You have been good neighbors all these years."

When Jane came to say good-by to Patty, she said, "I'll never want to pass this place again, without you here."

"And I'll miss you more than tongue can tell," Patty said again.

"Be sure to write to us once in a while," said Mrs. Marvin.

At last, Molly was tied behind the wagon, for they must take at least one cow to give them milk on the way and after they arrived at their

new home. The yoke had been placed on Buck
and Brindle, the oxen, and they had been hitched
to the wagon to draw it. Father helped Mother
up to the seat in front and then handed little
Mary Ann to her. Kanah and Patty jumped

The Departure

up on the wagon at the rear and Father climbed
up on the seat.

"I might as well ride now," he said. "There
will be plenty of places where the roads will be
bad and I can't."

They said good-by to Aunt Polly and Grandmother and Uncle Reuben and the Marvins;

[39]

and then they were off. The tears were running down Mother's face as they drove out of the yard. Even Patty and Kanah, who were looking forward to adventure on this journey, felt very sober as they saw the last of their loved home.

As they passed through the village, they saw many old friends and neighbors, who had gathered there to see them off.

"Here are some pies for you," said one friend, as she handed three mince pies up to Mother.

"Here is a pan of doughnuts," said another.

"And here is enough chicken for two or three meals," said another.

For Patty there were gifts of ribbon and a book and calico for a new dress.

"Good-by," they said, and waved their hands to the old friends, as they passed on through the village and disappeared around a bend toward the west.

"A fine family they are," said one man. "It is too bad we had to lose them from our community."

"A very fine family," said another. "I hope they will have good luck in their new home."

The slow oxen plodded along over the rough muddy spring road and Molly walked slowly behind the wagon all the rest of that day, till they stopped for the night beside the road, close to a clump of hemlock trees.

Kanah and Father collected some dry wood and made a fire, over which they boiled a kettle of water for tea. They rolled a log close to it, where Mother and Patty and Mary Ann could sit while they ate.

"Wasn't it good of Mrs. Smith to give us all this chicken ready cooked?" said Mother, as she passed it around.

"And these doughnuts taste mighty good," said Father, as he ate one that Mrs. Marvin had given them.

With some of Molly's good milk for the children and the refreshing hot tea for Father and Mother, they had their first supper in the open air, with the sun going down in the west and the first stars appearing in the sky over their heads.

"Whew! But that is a good supper," said Kanah.

"Food tastes good when you have been riding all day in crisp air," said Father.

"I was hungry enough to eat our pewter porringers," said Patty.

They kept the fire burning all that night. Mother and Patty and Mary Ann slept in the wagon, but Father and Kanah made a bed of hemlock boughs covered with blankets and a buffalo robe. It was the first night they had ever passed with no roof over their heads, but it was by no means to be the last.

CHAPTER VI

ON THE ROAD

I T was six days since they had left their home with its warm fires and good beds, its beautiful front door and the tasty meals that Mother had cooked in the kettles that hung from the crane.

By day the slow oxen had plodded along over the rough roads, often having to pull with all their might to drag the heavy wagon out of a mud-hole. They had come to many a place in the road where the melting snows on the hills and mountains had formed ponds that covered the roads from side to side.

"I declare these roads are worse than I imagined they could be this time of year," said Father. "We should have waited, I guess, till the weather was settled and spring thaws past."

Night was the hardest time, for sometimes a storm would come up and they would waken to find themselves shivering with cold.

Kanah and Patty minded the hardships the least of any of the family. Patty would curl up, with her head on a bag of meal, and sleep as soundly as in her bed back home. Kanah declared he would miss the stars over his head if he ever slept under a roof again.

It was Mother who felt the jolting and the jouncing most of all.

"It seems as if my bones would fall apart sometimes," she said. "And we fairly have to watch a tree to see whether we move or not."

"Watch a twee! Watch a twee!" echoed little Mary Ann.

"It is a tedious ride," said Father, "but just a few more miles and we'll come to a turnpike."

"What is a turnpike?" asked Patty.

"Don't you know?" asked Kanah, in a disdainful tone.

"Maybe you don't yourself," she said, tossing her head.

"I do," he declared. "A turnpike is a good road that doesn't have any ruts or bog-holes in it. Isn't it, Father?" he asked.

"I can't say there aren't any ruts or bog-holes," said Father, "but it is much better than these ordinary roads. You haven't told Patty very much about it, though. What else do you know?"

"Why, there is a tollgate every few miles, where folks have to pay toll."

"Why do they have to pay toll?" asked Patty.

Father did not answer that question at once,

but said, "When a country is new, there aren't any roads, you know."

"Oh, I know that," said Patty. "There are only forests everywhere."

"Yes," said Father, "and there are Indian paths through the forest. Then, when settlers come, they cut down the trees and make the path wide enough for a wagon, but it is still very rough, with stumps and stones and mud-holes in it."

"I know what next," put in Kanah. "After a while, they make it still wider and get out the stumps and the stones and fill up the hollows; and then there is a road like this one."

"I see you have been thinking, son," said Father. "You see this is none too good in the best of weather and it is very poor in bad weather. It costs money to make good roads, and so there are tollgates where people who use them have to pay for the privilege."

"But I don't see why it is called a turnpike," said Kanah.

"Then I'll tell you," said Father. "Sometimes, especially in the early days, there would actually be a pole or pike placed across the road, so a traveler could not pass till he had paid the toll. Then, when he had paid, the pike would be turned, so he could go on."

[45]

"Oh, I see," said Patty. "Turn the pike—turnpike."

"That is it," said Father, "but nowadays there is a house, called a tollgate, which stands at the side of the road and somebody is there to receive the toll."

"Will we have to pay toll?" asked Patty.

"We surely will," replied Father. "Before we get to the end of our journey, we will have to pay toll many times."

"I am sure I shall be glad when we do reach the turnpike," said Mother.

By the middle of the afternoon, they came to it. As the oxen swung onto it, the wheels did not creak so much, the riding was easier and they could go faster.

"We'll have this good turnpike all the way to Troy," said Father.

They had not been going far on it when Patty exclaimed, "What is that ahead of us?"

Indeed it did look strange to one who had never seen such a thing before, for there was a house beside the road, with a roof extending clear over the road.

"Oh, that is a tollgate," said Father, "our first tollgate. Here, Kanah, you may hand the toll to the man at the window."

He handed Kanah six cents. When they came opposite the tollgate, Kanah dropped the money into the man's hand and they were going on, when the man said, "That is not enough."

"That is what I paid last year when I went down to Troy," said Father.

"But you have a heavier load this time; and besides there is a cow walking along behind. Four cents more."

Father reached into his wallet and took out the four cents.

"I hope they don't all charge so much," he said. "We have to watch out for the pennies or we won't have enough to last till we get to the end of our journey."

"It is very handy having that roof over the road," said Mother. "If the sun were too hot, it would make a pleasant shade while folks pay their toll, and if it should be raining it would keep the rain off."

That night they camped by some woods at the side of the road. The ground in the woods was bright with spring flowers and a little brook sang merrily not far away to give them good water to drink. But a rain came up in the night and put out their camp fire. It sent Kanah and Father scurrying to the wagon for shelter and drenched Molly and the oxen. The wind blew cold and they all crowded under the cover of the wagon, trying to keep dry. And they were

[47]

all glad when the morning light shone in the eastern sky.

"It isn't so nice living in a wagon with no roof over our heads as I thought it would be," said Patty.

"You must not get tired of it so soon," said Father. "We have many long days to go yet and over three hundred miles to travel."

The second day after this, they came to the city of Troy, on the east side of a big river. Father drove to the center of town, where there were stores and blacksmith shops and many wagons on the main street.

"Where do I find the ferry?" he asked a man who was standing in front of one of the stores. When he had been told, he turned the oxen down a street leading to the river.

"What river is this that we have to cross?" he asked Patty.

"Why, it is the—" and she stopped to think what it might be.

"You don't know what river it is," said Kanah, who was eager to tell.

"I do, too," said Patty. "Is it the Mohawk River?" she guessed.

Father and Mother smiled. Kanah held up his hand, as he did in school when he wanted to answer a question.

"You may tell," said Father.

"The Hudson River," he promptly replied.

"But the Mohawk is here somewhere," said Patty. "I have seen it in my geography."

"It doesn't flow the same way," said Kanah. "We'll see that for a long part of our journey after we leave Albany."

"Right," said Father. "But here we are at the ferry."

The ferryboat was at the other side of the river, so they had to wait till it came back.

"What makes it go?" asked Patty, as they watched it coming toward them. "I don't see any sails on it."

"This boat doesn't have any sails," said Father.

"How *does* it go?" asked Kanah. "I don't see any smokestack, so it can't go by steam, as the big steamboats do."

"Keep your eyes open, both of you," said Father. "See if you can find out. It is made to go in rather a curious way."

The ferryboat soon came up to the dock and they drove onto it, Kanah leading Molly. Patty now climbed down and they both started to look around. As they did so, the ferryboat began to move out into the river. They could see the big paddle-wheels, one on each side of the boat, turning round and round in the water.

[49]

"But I can't see what makes them go," said Patty.

Kanah had spied something and he soon shouted to her, "Come here. I have found out."

Patty scrambled down over a railing. There was a horse walking on a wooden floor with grooves for his feet to step in. The horse walked steadily, but he did not get anywhere. He always stayed in the same place, because the floor under his feet moved backward.

"I don't see how that makes the boat move," said Patty.

But Kanah had guessed.

"See, there's another horse on the other side of the boat," he said. "They are both walking on a big flat wheel that we can't see much of, because it is under the deck, but they make it go round and round; and this wheel makes the two big paddle-wheels go round and round in the water."

They were now in the middle of the river. The city of Troy on the eastern bank was getting farther away each moment and the fields on the western bank were drawing nearer.

They now climbed up on the wagon. "I have found out," Kanah reported. "Horses make it go."

"They keep walking all the time," said Patty. "They don't get anywhere, but the boat does."

[50]

"It is something like a dog making a churn go," said Kanah.

"I think it is like the squirrel cage I once saw," said Patty.

"I am glad you used your eyes and your heads," said Father.

"I should think those horses would get tired of walking all day in the same place," said Mother.

"Oh, they don't seem to mind," said Kanah.

"There is one of these horse-ferries at Albany, too, I am told," said Father.

"Why didn't we go down there and cross on that one?" asked Kanah, who was never content till he had found out why everything was done.

"Well, I understand that there isn't a good road on the east side of the river," said Father. "By crossing here, we'll have a very good road the six miles down to Albany."

They had by this time reached the western side, and the horses stopped treading. Father drove the oxen off and Kanah followed, leading Molly, who showed her delight at being on land again by nibbling some wild flowers at the side of the river, until Kanah pulled her along and tied her to the rear of the wagon.

Then they started down to the city of Albany, about which they had heard so much and which they were so eager to see.

[51]

CHAPTER VII

THE WARNING

IF there had been any airplanes in the year 1823 and you had flown in one over the New England States, you would have seen on many of the roads white-covered wagons filled with household goods. In those wagons, if you could have looked under the canvas cover, you would have seen families from Massachusetts and Connecticut, from New Hampshire and Vermont, and some from Rhode Island and Maine. You would have noticed that they were all headed toward Albany.

The men in those wagons wanted some of that new fertile land, about which they had heard so much. They were willing to work hard, to chop down the trees of the forest, to dig up the tough stubborn roots, to endure great hardships in order that they might make a good home there for their families.

The land to which they were all going was that portion of New York State west of the Genesee River. It touches Lake Ontario on the north, the Niagara River and Lake Erie on the west and the State of Pennsylvania on the south. People spoke of it as "The Genesee Country," or as "Western New York."

Twenty years before this, with the exception of some settlers on the Niagara River and along the Ridge Road, this country was a vast forest, through which roamed wild animals and which neither plow nor hoe had ever touched. No fields of grain were there, no orchards or gardens or flower-beds.

By this year 1823, here and there in that vast forest a settler had built a log cabin; here and there were several log houses close together; but there was still room for thousands of strong, hardy men to come and chop down trees and clear the land, for brave women to live, to cook and to spin, to weave the cloth and make their clothes, to teach their children and to endure the hardships that pioneers must face.

So the wagon in which Kanah and Patty were riding was not the only one coming into Albany that April day. Indeed, when they turned up the main street, they saw dozens of covered wagons and oxcarts hitched along the street or going westward up the hill on which the State

House stood; for Albany was then, as now, the capital of the State of New York. Not only were there covered wagons on that street, but there were stagecoaches and peddlers' carts and many fine carriages in which rode rich and fashionable ladies.

Patty's eyes sparkled, for in all her life she had never gone to any place larger than the little village near their home, with its one store, its white church, its schoolhouse and its few houses.

"Oh, what a lot of stores!" she said. "Can't we stop here a while? I want to go into some of the stores and see the pretty things."

"Yes, we are going to stop for an hour or two," said Father. "I have to attend to some business here. I want to get a plowpoint and a new axe and a few other things. While I am doing those things, the rest of you may look around."

He drove up State Street two or three blocks and then turned onto a side street. State Street was a very wide street, with sidewalks and a pavement, but this side street was not paved and pigs were running around in the muddy roadway.

Father tied the oxen to a hitching-post and left Molly tied to the rear of the wagon.

"What do you want to do while I am gone

on my errands?" Father asked Mrs. Armstrong.

"I would like to go into one or two of the stores," she said. "I'd like to see the beautiful things in them; and then if only I could go into one of these inns and rest in a rocking-chair. I can't think of anything I'd like better."

"That can be managed," said Father. "Here is a hotel right down at the corner. You might get a cup of tea and a slice of toast and then sit in one of the rocking-chairs till the rest of us come back."

"And I'll keep Mary Ann with me," she said. "But first I'll take Patty to one of the stores."

"Oh, can't I go into more than one?" asked Patty.

"Well, now," said Father, "when Mother is through looking in the one store, there is no reason why Kanah can't go with you anywhere you want to go. He is old enough to do that."

"Oh, shucks!" said Kanah. "I wanted to go down to the river and see the big steamer that comes up from New York. I don't want to go to stores."

"See here, son," said Father, "you are big enough to do some things even if you don't care especially about them. Do as I say—go with Patty to see the things that interest her. And watch out that no harm comes to her."

"Maybe I had better stay with her instead of

coming back to rest in a rocking-chair," said Mother.

"No such thing," said Father. "You need that rest. We'll all meet here in about two hours. If I am not back here by that time, I'll come as soon as I can."

Albany

The four of them—Kanah and Patty, Mother and Mary Ann—went back to State Street. It was a bustling street, with the covered wagons and stagecoaches, with the two-wheeled ox-carts, the one-horse carriages and the two-horse carriages and the peddlers' carts. They walked down a block and came to a dry-goods store.

Mrs. Armstrong and Patty could scarcely leave the counter where the dress goods were— silks and velvets of lovely colors, satins and cassimeres of lovely colors. Patty saw a piece of merino just the color of her best dress. That reminded her to look down at her own plain dress of homespun, for which Mother had woven the cloth herself.

"Oh, Mother, I wish we had put on our best dresses," she said. "See how nicely these ladies are dressed."

She was looking at some fashionable ladies at one of the counters. Indeed, in their heavy silks and large bonnets trimmed with flowers, they did look very grand.

"Our dresses will do very well," replied Mother. "Though it would have been nice, just once on our journey, to have put on our best ones. But there are many ladies and girls dressed just as we are, so no one will think it strange."

When they were ready to leave that store, Mother said, "Now I'll go back to the inn and rest. Where is Kanah?"

They found him just outside the door, watching the busy scene. He and Patty started down the street. Patty's eyes fairly glowed as she went into this store and that. Then, to please Kanah, she went into a hardware store where he wanted to look at the jackknives. Before they knew it, the time was nearly up, but Patty saw one more sign that made her eager to go into yet another store. It was that of the jewelry store of Joseph T. Rice, at the corner of State Street and South Market Street.

Kanah went willingly this time, for he felt sure that this store would have some watches. So they went in together and stood looking at the watches and the clocks and the rings while the jeweler waited on a customer. There were strings of gold beads also, among the other beautiful things.

"Oh, Kanah, see those beads," said Patty. "They are almost exactly like mine."

"They look like yours," he said. "But I'll bet they aren't as nice," he added loyally.

"Of course not," said Patty.

"I wish I had one of those watches," said Kanah.

The jeweler came over to them now. "Would you like to look at something?" he asked.

"I would like to look at the watches," said Kanah. "I can't buy one, though."

"Look at them all you want to," said the jeweler, as he placed two watches on the counter —a plain one and a repeating one.

"This repeating one is interesting," said the

[58]

jeweler. "Just press the little spring in the edge of it and notice what happens."

Kanah pressed the spring and the watch softly struck the hour that had just passed.

"Oh! I'd like to have one of them," he said.

"May I see the beads a little closer?" asked Patty.

The jeweler took one of the strings of beads out of the box and laid it down before her. Patty looked eagerly at the round shining beads.

"I have a string just like these," she said. "Only mine are a bit bigger, and they have initials on the clasp."

"But these are solid gold," said the jeweler.

"Mine are solid gold," said Patty.

"How much do you charge for that string?" asked Kanah, who always wanted to know the price of things.

"That string is fifty dollars," said the man.

"Whew!" said Kanah, ending with a whistle.

"Oh! Are mine worth as much as that?" asked Patty.

"Yes, if they are really solid gold. Where are yours? I'll tell you how much they are worth."

"They are in our covered wagon," said Kanah.

"They are in a little leather trunk in the wagon," added Patty.

"You don't mean that you left a string of gold beads in a covered wagon!" exclaimed the jeweler. "That was a risky thing to do. There is apt to be somebody around, watching his chance to steal from these covered wagons. There is hardly ever anything in them that a person would want to steal, but a string of gold beads— well, if I were you, I'd go right back and look after them."

"Oh! We never thought of that," said Kanah.

"Thank you for showing us your nice jewelry," said Patty. "We'll hurry back to the wagon."

And they rushed out the door.

"This way," said Kanah. "I remember just where the wagon is."

As they hurried along, they ran into a peddler's pack and knocked it off from his back, sending the things flying in all directions.

"Oh, we are so sorry," said Patty, as they stopped to gather up the needles and thread and buttons and other things that were scattered around.

They helped him place them all in the pack and then they started on, a little more slowly. They watched their chance to cross the street and came to the side street where the wagon had been left. Just as they turned into it, a man jumped down from the wagon and ran off.

[60]

"Oh, dear! Oh, dear!" cried Patty.

Such a sight as met their eyes when she and Kanah climbed up. The little trunk was open, its lid lying against the canvas. Their best clothes were scattered over the bags and bundles; and the sea-shells were lying on the feather beds.

"Are the beads safe?" asked Patty, as Kanah climbed in first.

"No; there isn't a thing left in the trunk," he replied.

"Oh, dear me!" groaned Patty. "And I was never going to part with them."

"You ought not to have left them," said Kanah.

It wasn't often that Patty cried. Father and Mother had frequently noticed that she wasn't a girl to make a fuss over anything that couldn't be helped. But now she burst into tears, and sobbed as they went into the hotel to find Mother.

"Why, Patty, what is the matter?" asked Mother.

"My beads have been stolen," she replied.

"Somebody has taken everything out of the little trunk and the beads are gone," said Kanah.

"And I'll never see them again," sobbed Patty.

"Don't cry any more," said Mother. "The

beads are all safe. But who has been in our wagon?"

She reached into her pocket and took out the beads.

"Oh, goody! Oh, thank you, Mother!" cried Patty. "How did you happen to have them?"

"While I was sitting here, it came to me that it was not a safe place to leave them, so I went to the wagon and got them."

"Oh, thank you! I'll never forget them again," declared Patty.

When Father came back a little later, he said, "I bought this light axe for you, son. You can learn to do many useful things with it. Perhaps you can help build the—"

"Oh, Father, a thief has been in our wagon," broke in Patty.

"A thief!" he exclaimed. "What did he steal? I hope he didn't carry off your beads."

"No, he didn't. Mother had them safe," said Patty. "But he threw all the things out of the trunk."

"I was going to take you and Kanah down to see the steamboat," said Father, "but the wagon must not be left alone any longer."

So they all went back to the wagon and carefully looked things over to see whether anything was missing.

"Everything seems to be safe," said Father.

"Patty and I scared the thief away," said Kanah, proudly.

"I'll stay with the wagon while you three go to the steamboat," said Mother.

Father then took Kanah and Patty down to the dock to see the big steamboat that had come up from New York.

"It is like a palace, as you can see," said the man who took them over it. "And the speed it makes! Why, we came up from New York in fourteen hours."

"That is wonderful," said Father.

"Yes, sir," said the man. "In fourteen hours we made that trip of a hundred and sixty miles; and without a sail up. Mr. Robert Fulton did a grand thing when he invented the steamboat."

Patty thought it was very wonderful that the boat could go a hundred and sixty miles in fourteen hours, when they could go only twelve or fifteen miles a day behind their slow oxen.

They went back to the wagon. Mother had already picked up the dresses and the sea-shells and put them back in the little trunk. They all climbed into the wagon and started up State street, out the Western Road past the beautiful State House that stood on the hill. They camped that night half way to the Mohawk River.

[63]

CHAPTER VIII

THE TURNPIKE

T HE Mohawk River rises in the central part of New York and flows in an easterly direction for more than a hundred miles, until it empties into the Hudson. Along the north bank of that river there ran the Mohawk Turnpike, the best road leading from Albany into that new country to which the Armstrong family were going. Along this turnpike there was a tollgate every few miles, where every passing vehicle had to pay a few pennies for toll.

It was along this turnpike that the thousands of covered wagons which had traveled the roads of the New England States toward Albany proceeded on their way to the "Genesee Country." On a certain day of that April, 1823, along this turnpike went the wagon in which Patty and Kanah were riding.

"Well, we won't see another large city for a good long time," said Mother, the second day after they had left Albany.

"That's a fact," said Father. "But there will

be plenty of other interesting things to see."

Along this road stagecoaches were speeding, drawn by four or six horses, with the passengers inside the coach and the driver on the seat in front. Every once in a while Patty and Kanah would hear the sound of a horn and soon horses and coach would go flying past them.

"They go like lightning," said Kanah.

"That is stretching it a bit," said Father. "Maybe they go eight miles an hour, though."

"I wish we could go as fast as that," said Patty.

"We can't go any faster than the oxen can walk," said Father.

"And we mustn't hurry Molly, either," said Mother. "She must think it very strange to be kept going day after day, with no chance to eat from a manger or to browse in a meadow."

One day, as they were eating their dinner of boiled potatoes and fried ham and buckwheat pancakes, cooked over a fire at the side of the road, a string of ten covered wagons came along, one behind the other.

"I wonder why so many come together," said Kanah.

"Let's find out," said Father.

He and Kanah went to one of the wagons and Father said to the driver, "How do you

[65]

do? We have been wondering why so many of you are going along together."

"We are all from one village," the man replied. "All of us decided to go west."

"Well, well!" said Mr. Armstrong. "What an idea! A whole village moving west!"

"Why not?" said the man. "It is much pleasanter than going alone. We have been neighbors and we'll be neighbors in our new home. It is very handy to have other wagons along. If one of us gets stuck in the mud, the others can help get his wagon out."

"A very good idea," said Father. "Though we haven't had to be pulled out of the mud yet."

"Wait till you get farther on," said the man. "There are some pretty bad roads on ahead, I hear."

The ten wagons passed on along the road. The Armstrong family put out their fire and went on their way.

Across on the south bank of the Mohawk, they could see huge piles of dirt and heaps of stones.

"What are all those piles of stones for?" asked Kanah.

"They have been dug out to make the new canal," Father replied. "You have heard of the Erie Canal. It is sometimes called Governor Clinton's Big Ditch."

"But I didn't know it was near this place," said Kanah.

"I know about it," said Patty. "It is a long canal being dug from the Hudson River to Lake Erie, clear across the State."

"And boats are going to be drawn along it by horses walking on the towpath," added Kanah.

"A part of it is done now," said Father, "but not as far as we are going."

"I wish it were all done now," said Mother. "I expect when it is done, folks will go in boats and not have this long tiresome journey in a jolting wagon."

Mother did not often mention being tired. Father looked at her face and thought, "It is a long journey for a gentle woman to take."

The road was fairly good here. Sometimes they passed farmhouses, with tilled fields and pasture lands around them. Sometimes they went through tiny villages. Sometimes they went through long stretches of forest. Every eight or ten miles they came to a tollgate and had to give up some pennies.

Sometimes they came to corduroy roads and the wagon bumped along over the logs. Sometimes they came to rivers and creeks which they crossed on bridges. But sometimes they came to a little stream of water where there was no bridge. Then there was nothing to do but drive

[67]

down one bank, through the water, and up the opposite bank. It wasn't always an easy thing to do.

Now, all this time the precious string of beads was resting safely in the little leather trunk. Once in a while Patty would open the trunk and take them out to look at them.

She liked to ride at the rear of the wagon, where she could jump down when she was tired of riding. She would walk a while and then swing up again. It was just after she had swung up onto the wagon, one day, that she decided to take the beads out and wear them for a while. She had reached over and opened the trunk and taken the beads out of their box, when Father stopped the oxen on the bank of a little stream of water, which a rain had made higher than usual.

"Here's a pretty bad stream to ford," Father said to Kanah. "You may untie Molly and lead her across after the wagon."

The oxen went down the bank into the water, which came up to their knees. The wagon wheels went into the water and sank in the mud so that it was hard for the oxen to pull it. But finally they reached the opposite bank and began to go up.

"Hold on tight," said Father.

It was then that Patty forgot the beads in her

[68]

lap, as she grabbed hold of the side of the wagon to keep from slipping into the water.

"Get up, Buck. Get up, Brindle," said Father, as he urged them up the incline.

The patient beasts pulled with all their might and soon had the wagon at the top of the bank.

"Whoa, Buck. Whoa, Brindle," said Father, when they were on level ground again.

The bundles and bags and household goods had slipped around while they were going down the one bank and up the other; so Father began to put the things back in place.

"I hope we won't have to cross many streams as bad as that," said Mother.

As Kanah waded through the water, leading Molly, he was soaked nearly to the hips. But everything in the wagon appeared to be safe.

Suddenly Patty exclaimed, "Oh, my beads! My beads!"

"Your beads? What is the matter with them?" asked Mother.

"They are gone," she answered.

"Your beads gone?" said Father. "What were you doing with them?"

"I had them in my hands when we started to cross that stream. I am afraid they dropped into the water."

"I'll go back and look," Kanah offered.

[69]

He was already drenched but walked into the stream and began to search the place where they had crossed. He reached down into the water here and there, but did not touch anything that felt like beads.

"Oh, why did I take them out of the trunk?" moaned Patty.

"There is no use in crying over spilt milk,"

Loss of the Beads

said Father. "If we don't find them—why, you'll just have to be brave about it."

"When did you have them last?" asked Mother. "Did you have them when the wagon reached this bank?"

Patty thought a moment. "Yes, I'm sure I did, for when Father said, 'Hold on tight,' I remember that I had just put them down in my lap."

[70]

"That shows that they are near this bank of the stream," said Father.

They went back and forth over every bit of ground and put their hands down into the water. Just as they had given up the search and were starting back to the wagon, Kanah shouted, "Here they are!"

"Oh, goody! Goody!" laughed Patty, as she turned and ran back. There was Kanah, standing in a foot of water and holding up the string of beads, all dripping and muddy.

"Where did you find them?" asked Mother.

"At the bottom of the stream," he answered. "They had sunk into the mud."

Then he said to Patty, "I said you would lose them. Don't you remember?"

"I remember," she replied. "Thank you very much, Kanah, for finding them. And I'll never be careless with them again."

"You had better not take them out again when the wagon is in motion," said Mother.

The mud was easily washed off and Patty put the treasure back in the little leather trunk.

CHAPTER IX

PATTY'S IDEA

THE second day after this, the weather turned cold in the middle of the night. The rain descended suddenly and put out the fire which Father was keeping to ward off wild animals. They had come to a wilder country, where the woods were more dense and the settlers were farther apart.

Suddenly the rain began to pour on Father and Kanah, who were sleeping on a pile of blankets on the ground. They quickly moved their bed to a spot under the wagon. The wind came up and shook the flaps of the canvas top and blew the rain inside.

"What is the matter?" asked Patty, when she was awakened by something cold and moist on her face.

"Rain," Mother answered. "A hard storm has come up."

Mother tried to fasten the curtains at the front, so the rain couldn't come in. All the while she was shivering in the cold wind.

Father came up to the front of the wagon.

"I'll fasten the curtains," he said. "You had better keep inside, out of the rain."

Mother was glad to climb back to the middle of the wagon, where the rain couldn't reach. Still she couldn't get warm, though she pulled the blankets and quilts around her.

"And this is what it means to be a pioneer," she was thinking, as she lay awake. But did she say it to Father or any one else? What she did say in the morning was, "I think I'll be better before the day is over."

Father, however, saw that she was ill. Patty could see it, too, so she tried to do things that would make Mother more comfortable. She tucked the bedding in, so as to keep the cold out. She amused Mary Ann, so that Mother could sleep.

"We'd better go on," said Father, after they had eaten a cold breakfast. "We won't get any wetter moving than we will staying here, and perhaps we'll find some place where there is more protection from the weather."

They tied Molly to the rear of the wagon and started on. The wagon jolted over the rough roads. The wheels went down into a deep rut every few minutes. To make matters worse, they had not been going two hours before it became so cold that the rain formed into ice as fast as it fell.

[73]

"Such weather I never saw in April," said Father.

"How do you feel, Mother?" asked Patty.

She tried to say that she was not very sick, but she could not deceive them.

"If we can only come to an inn, I am going to get a warm room for you," said Father, "and you shall stay there till you are well."

At this, Mother roused up. "Oh, you mustn't do that. We must not waste money on things we can do without. I'll be all right just as soon as the storm is over."

After a while they did come in sight of an inn. Father started to drive in, but Mother protested, saying, "No, don't drive in, please. I'll be all right soon."

They went on past the inn for a quarter of a mile and there stopped in the edge of some woods.

"I'll get something that will make Mother feel better," said Father. "You children stay here with her and watch the fire and the cattle. I am going to see if I can't shoot a rabbit or a wild duck to make some broth for her. This food that we have been eating isn't good for a sick person."

He shouldered his gun and hurried off through the woods. Mary Ann was tired of staying in the wagon, so she now begged to be taken down to the ground.

"All right," said Kanah, as he lifted her down. "What with the fire and the cattle and everything, I can't look out for her, so you'll have to," he said to Patty.

But Patty meanwhile had been doing some thinking. "I wish I had some money. I wish I did have some money. I know what I would do with it."

Then, all at once, something flashed into her mind.

"I'll do it. I will. I will," she decided.

She went to the back of the wagon, swung up into it and quietly reached into the little leather trunk and took something out of it—something which she slipped into the pocket of her dress. She went to Kanah, who was now dragging a piece of wood to the fire.

"Kanah, you stay with Mother and watch out for Mary Ann," she whispered. "I'll be back before long."

"Where are you going?" he asked.

"Just up to the inn. I have a plan," she replied. "If Mother misses me, don't tell her where I have gone."

"You had better not go there alone," protested Kanah. "You had better not."

But Patty was running up the road toward the

inn. Kanah did not dare to call after her, for fear of waking Mother. As he couldn't leave Mary Ann and the cattle and the fire, he watched her turn into the yard of the inn and wondered what she was planning to do.

CHAPTER X

FIVE DOLLARS

JUST as Patty ran into the yard of the inn, a stagecoach came rumbling up, drawn by four swift horses. The driver drew up to the steps of the inn and stopped the horses.

"Have the fresh teams hitched on in ten minutes," he said to the hostler, who came out to change horses. "I'll get a bite to eat."

Some of the passengers got out, for they were at the end of their journey. Other people came out of the inn to take their places in the coach. The hostler unhitched the four horses and took them back to the barn at the rear of the hotel. He soon appeared with four other horses and hitched them to the stagecoach.

Patty did not wait to see all this, for she was eager to attend to the errand on which she had come. She went up the steps and into a large room—the parlor it was called. There was much commotion and noise there, as the travelers who had just come on the stagecoach with their portmanteaus and bandboxes took up much space; and the people who were to go on the stagecoach with their portmanteaus and bandboxes also took up much space. And they were all talking at once.

Patty stood looking around to see whether she could tell which one was the innkeeper. After several minutes, she made up her mind that he was the short man with the red face, to whom some people were paying their bills and from whom others were trying to find out where their rooms were or what time dinner would be ready.

As she stood there, she noticed a well-dressed gentleman and his wife standing in the center of the room, surrounded by a number of pieces of baggage. They were evidently about to start on, for Patty heard the man say to the hostler, "Bring my horses up to the door as soon as you can manage, Bill."

"Yes, sir," the hostler answered, "just as soon as the stage gets away."

After a few more minutes, the people going in the stagecoach had all left the room. The well-dressed man and his wife were sitting in front of the fireplace, toasting their feet before starting off.

Patty now went up to the innkeeper and said, "Please, sir, wouldn't you like to buy a string of gold beads?"

She held them out for him to see, hoping that he would say "Yes," and yet afraid that he would say it and that she would have to give them up at once.

"Wouldn't I like to buy a string of gold beads?" he said. "Well, now, I hadn't been counting on doing any such foolish thing."

"They are very nice beads," Patty pleaded. "They are solid gold."

He took them out of the box and held them up and viewed them at arm's length.

"They do look like nice beads," he said. "They are very pretty. They would look well on your pretty neck. Then why do you want to sell them?"

"My mother is sick and I want to get some money to pay for a warm room and a bed for her," Patty answered.

"Your mother is sick? Where is she?"

"Down the road by the woods, in a covered wagon," replied Patty.

"Sick—and in a covered wagon on a day like this!" he exclaimed.

Then, turning to the man at the fireplace, he remarked, "Ain't it dreadful that frail women, as this girl's mother must be, are traveling about in all sorts of weather, with no heat and no roof over their heads but thin canvas? But thousands of them are doing it these days. Brave, that's what I call 'em."

"I agree with you," said the man. "It is hard enough for strong men to take these journeys in covered wagons, to say nothing about women and children doing it."

Then he turned to Patty. "I'll warrant you have been on the road a good number of days already. Where are you from?"

"We have been traveling ten days already and we came from Vermont," said Patty—"from a place near the Green Mountains."

"I can make a guess as to where you are going," said the innkeeper. "You are on your way to the Genesee Country. Ain't you? What is your name, child?"

"Patience Armstrong, but I am always called Patty."

"Ain't you folks going to Western New York, Patty?"

"Yes, sir," she replied, "but how did you know it?" She could not remember having mentioned it.

"How do I know it? Because all the folks that come past here in covered wagons these days are on their way to that place. Hundreds of those wagons have gone by in the last few months."

At this the woman spoke up. "What possesses folks to want to leave their homes in a civilized part of the country to go out there in the forest and live among wild beasts and have no comforts of life, is more than I can tell. For myself, I couldn't be hired to do it."

"That is my opinion," said the innkeeper. "Now, I and my wife are not folks for having lots of fine clothes and fine furniture and such foolish things, but we don't see why we shouldn't live where there is some comfort in living. We are not fond of mosquitoes and fever-and-ague and living in a dark log house and having no neighbors."

Patty had not thought of it in this way before. She didn't stop to think much about it now, before she spoke up, saying, "But doesn't some one have to be the first to go to a new country and live without neighbors?"

"Bravely spoke," said the innkeeper. "There have to be pioneers in every new land, and I suppose they ought to have a lot of credit for being willing to go through all those hardships."

"Well, I am willing to let some one else have the job," said the woman.

Though Patty was interested in this talk and it set her to thinking about the matter, when she

remembered it a few hours later, she was eager
now to finish the errand on which she had come
and get back to her mother. So she asked tim-
idly, "Will you buy the beads, sir?"

"Well, well! I nearly forgot all about the
beads, but I see you didn't forget."

Patty waited for his answer. "I am sorry,
Patty, but I can't buy them," he said. "We have
no use for fine jewelry. We have no little girl to
wear them and my wife doesn't care for gewgaws. But I'll let your mother come here, since
she is sick, and stay without pay for a day or
two, till she gets better."

Patty hesitated. "Oh, thank you very much,"
she said. "But I am sure she wouldn't do that.
She is proud. We don't beg."

"Oh, I see," said the innkeeper, looking with
admiration at Patty. "I'll go and talk it over
with my wife."

He went into another room. As Patty stood
there waiting, the man at the fireplace stepped
up to her and asked, "May I see the beads?"

Patty held out the box in which they lay. He
looked at them and then showed them to his
wife.

"They look like pretty good beads to me," he
said. "Maybe we had better buy them."

The wife took them over to a window, pre-
tending to want to see them better, but what

she really wanted was to say something to her husband without Patty's hearing it.

"They are expensive beads. Solid gold, I am sure," she said in a low tone. "Buy them; but you had better not pay very much for them.

Five Dollars

They must be an heirloom. See those lovely initials on the clasp."

The man came back to Patty. "I'll give you five dollars for them," he said.

"Five dollars isn't nearly as much as the jeweler at Albany said they were worth," she thought. "But maybe I can't get any more."

[83]

Then she replied, "Very well. You may have them for that."

The man gave her the five dollars and handed the beads to his wife, who placed them in one of the portmanteaus she was to take with her.

Just then the innkeeper came back. With the money safe in her pocket, Patty said to him, "I have sold my beads to this gentleman. Now I'd like to see a room, a nice room, for my mother."

"Come and I'll show you the best one we have empty," he said.

It was a large room, with windows on two sides, with a huge double bed and a fireplace. Patty hoped the bed was a comfortable one. Then it suddenly occurred to her that she might not have money enough.

"How much will it cost?" she asked.

"A dollar and a half a day, with meals," he replied.

Patty breathed a sigh of relief. "There is enough to keep Mother here three days, at least," she thought.

"I'll take it," she said. "We'll bring her here soon." Then she hurried back to the wagon.

"Patty Armstrong, where have you been all this time?" asked Kanah. "Mother has been asking for you. She has worried so much it has made her worse. Part of the time she doesn't talk sense. She must be pretty sick to be out of her head."

"Oh, I should have hurried," thought Patty. "But it took those men so long to make up their minds."

She climbed up into the wagon. "Here I am, Mother," she said.

"Oh, Patty, where have you been all this time?" Mother asked.

"I have been to the inn," Patty replied, "and you are to go there and have a good room and a real bed."

"Go to the inn? Oh, no," Mother protested. "We must save our money for the time when we shall need every dollar of it."

Her head was clear now and she was talking sense. "I'll be all right. I'll be better to-morrow."

Patty could see that Mother was feverish and that she coughed frequently.

"But you are really to go," she insisted.

"Where will we get the money to pay for it?" asked Mother.

"I have sold my beads for enough," said Patty.

"Sold your gold beads?" exclaimed Mother. "You shouldn't have done that. Your precious beads that you think so much of. You said you would never part with them."

[85]

"I wanted you to have a good warm place to sleep," said Patty.

"Oh, dear!" said Mother. "What sacrifices folks have to make who go to settle a new country!"

It was the only time she was heard to complain during all that long journey and through all the years of hardship after they reached the new country.

Just then Father came back, bringing a wild duck he had shot. As he came up to the wagon to ask how Mother was, she said, "What do you think our Patty has done? Sold her string of gold beads!"

"Sold your beads? Why, Patty, I am disappointed in you. Why did you do such a foolish thing?"

But when he knew the reason, he said, "Ah! That couldn't have been an easy thing to do. How much did you get for them?"

"Five dollars," she replied.

"But that wasn't nearly what they are worth," said he.

"I know, but I couldn't get any more," said Patty.

"We are going to buy them back," said Mother. "Let's hurry to the inn."

Leaving Kanah in charge of the cow and the fire, the rest of them got into the wagon and drove back to the inn. Father helped Mother into the parlor and she said to the innkeeper, "Where is the man who bought Patty's string of gold beads? We'll give him his money back, for we want her to keep them. I am better and can stay in the wagon."

"I'm sorry, ma'am, but he left here just after she did, on his way to Albany, behind a span of fast horses."

CHAPTER XI

THE INN

"HOW good it seems to be in a room once more, with a roof over one's head to keep the rain off and a fire in the fireplace to keep it warm," said Mother, a few minutes later, as she sat toasting her feet before the fire, while Patty filled a warming-pan with coals and warmed the bed for her.

"I never thought much about a roof before," said Patty, as she poked the warming-pan into all corners of the bed.

"And isn't it wonderful to have a good bed to lie in?" said Mother, a few minutes after that, when she was lying in the big comfortable bed and Patty had tucked the warm covers around her.

The room had a big fireplace in which a fire was kept briskly burning by a servant who put a fresh log on every little while. A picture of Lafayette hung over the mantel. On the opposite wall was a picture of Washington.

Father waited to see that Mother was comfortable; then he said to Patty, "I'll go back where Kanah is. You may stay here a while; and then you had better come down there, you and Mary Ann. Kanah and I will have dinner ready for you."

He was turning to go when the innkeeper's wife came up.

"Patty and her little sister may stay in the room, too," she said. "There will be no extra charge. Here is a big couch for them to sleep on. And we won't charge them very much for meals," she said.

"Well, that is very kind," said Father. "Very kind, indeed."

"Patty may make herself useful by bringing drinks of water to her mother and carrying her meals up and telling us when the fire needs fixing," she added.

"Would you like to stay here, Patty?" asked Father.

"Oh, that would be great fun," said Patty, "and I'll take care of Mary Ann, too."

So it was agreed. And as Father left, he said, "Kanah or I will come up a few times every day to see how Mother is."

After a dinner of hot soup, Mother went to sleep, and slept all that long afternoon.

"I feel better already," she said, on waking.

As for Patty, she loved to go down to the parlor and watch the travelers come and go.

She liked to watch a stagecoach come swinging up to the steps, its four horses glad to be at the end of their trip. She liked to see the passengers get out, with all their bandboxes and portmanteaus and leather trunks. Most of all she liked to hear them talk by the fireplace.

"Isn't it astonishing how many of those covered wagons are going west these days?" said a man on the second evening.

"Would you believe it, I saw fifteen hundred of them go past here last winter," said the innkeeper. "Yes, sir, I counted them. Fifteen hundred."

By the middle of the third day, Mother declared she felt well enough to go on. Indeed she looked so much rested and she seemed so well that Patty would willingly have parted with another string of beads if it had been necessary.

"Good-by. Good luck to you in that new country," said the innkeeper, as they were ready to start off.

"We shall never forget your kindness and that of your wife," said Mother.

They started on west, with Molly tied to the rear of the wagon, as she had been all the way along. They started on west, with nearly two hundred miles yet to travel before they would reach that distant part of the State to which they planned to go.

CHAPTER XII

THE BOG-HOLES

"GET up, Buck. Get up, Brindle," Father shouted to the oxen.

The faithful animals tried to go ahead and pull the wagon out of the mud-hole in which it was stuck, but not an inch did it stir, for it had sunk into the mud almost up to the hubs of the wheels.

They had been on the road more than a week since leaving the inn. All these days they had been going slowly west behind the plodding oxen. Sometimes they passed farms, with clearings in which there were fields of wheat showing fresh and green after the winter. Sometimes they passed fields plowed for the summer crops of barley or corn or buckwheat. Then again there would be a long stretch of forest, for the country was getting wilder all the time and they were coming to that new part which was little more than one vast forest.

It was in one of these stretches of forest that they found themselves stuck in a bog-hole. Father jumped out into the mud and urged the oxen again.

[91]

"Get up, Buck. Get up, Brindle. Come now, both together, pull."

But although they pulled and strained with all their might, the wagon did not move.

"Will we have to stay here always?" asked Patty, from her perch on a pile of quilts.

"Maybe we'll sink down to China instead," said Kanah.

"China isn't down in the earth," protested Patty.

" 'Tis, too," said Kanah. "Way down on the other side of the earth. Right down beneath our feet."

"Could we sink down there?" asked Patty, with a troubled look.

"We aren't in any danger of going down as far as that," said Mother, "but we are in danger of staying here a good long time if someone doesn't come along to pull us out."

Kanah managed to climb out and jump across the deepest of the mud, but Patty and Mother and Mary Ann stayed there for an hour, till another wagon came in sight around the bend. This one was drawn by four horses. The driver stopped a few rods back.

"What is the trouble?" he asked.

"We're stuck," Father replied. "A terrible bog-hole here."

"I'll help you out," said the man.

[92]

He unhitched his four horses from their own wagon and hitched them to the Armstrong wagon. Even the four of them had to pull over and over again, but at last the wagon began to move and was soon safe out of the bog-hole.

"Thank you very much," said Father. "We might have had to stay here all night if you had not been willing to give us a lift."

"We all ought to help each other," said the man. "In a new country like this we are going to, maybe you'll have a chance to lend a hand to some one else."

"I hope so," said Father, "and I wish you the best of luck, wherever you are going."

"After we cross the Genesee River, which is only about eighty miles ahead, we are going twenty miles farther, along the Ridge Road. Then we intend to turn down toward Lake Ontario," replied the man. "Where are you going?"

"My land lies in Niagara County. We are going along the Ridge Road, too, but at least forty miles farther than you. Then we'll turn south," said Mr. Armstrong.

The man drove around the bog-hole and was on his way.

"What is this Ridge Road you were talking about?" asked Kanah.

"Well, suppose we wait till we get to it, where

[93]

you can see it, and then I'll tell you what I know," said Father.

In a few days, they had come to the village of Rochester. Mr. Armstrong took one of the bags of wheat to a grist mill and had it ground into flour. They saw the beautiful Falls of the Genesee, then they crossed the Genesee River on a bridge and before long found themselves on the Ridge Road.

"Why is it called the Ridge Road?" asked Patty.

"Just look at it," said Father, "and look off on each side of it. What do you see?"

"Why, it is a good road," said Patty.

"The land slopes down on each side of it," said Kanah. "We are on the top of a ridge of land."

"That is it," said Father, "and I am told that this ridge goes all the way to the Niagara River, over seventy miles. It is sandy, you see. They say it dries quickly, so there is never a bog-hole here."

"Well, that is nice," said Mother. "And isn't it lucky for us pioneers, too?"

"Indeed it is," said Father, "and I expect we'll find many settlers along this road."

They had not gone many miles before the sun was setting. Just as they were looking for a place to camp, where there would be good water for drinking, they came in sight of a log cabin, with a little clearing around it.

"Probably there is a well or a spring there," said Faith. "You may take the water jug and run up there, Kanah, and ask whether we can have some water."

Kanah ran up to the log house. It was not long before he came running back, carrying his jug as if it were empty.

"Do you suppose they are so mean they won't let us have any water?" said Patty.

But as soon as he came near, Kanah said, "Those folks are awfully nice. They have a deep well and a watering-trough where the cattle can drink and they want us to camp right in their yard."

"Well, now, that is kind," said Mother.

As they drove into the yard, a woman came to the door and a girl about Patty's age stood just outside.

"The water in our well is very pure and good," said the woman. "Use all you want of it."

At that moment a boy about Kanah's age appeared around the corner of the cabin.

"I'll help you draw it," he said.

He and Kanah let the bucket down into the well by the long sweep and drew up a bucket of clear cold water. They poured that into the jug for drinking and then drew up more for the watering-trough.

"We'd be glad to have you folks come in and eat supper with us," said the woman, whose name was Mrs. Castleton. "I have a pot of beans baking in the oven and some fresh loaves of bread and some dried-apple pies."

"Wouldn't those taste good?" thought Mother.

"Thank you," she said. "I'd like to furnish part of the supper, though. I have some good ham and some buckwheat flour and some fine maple syrup."

So the two families, who had been strangers to each other only an hour before, had a sociable time at supper, and Mother had a rocking-chair in which to rest.

"Why don't you settle here?" asked Mr. Castleton. "This is very good land."

"I wish you would," said the girl. "I'd like to have Patty live near by."

"It would be splendid," said the wife. "I would like some good neighbors."

"This does look like a good place," said Father, "and I am sure we would like you folks for neighbors, but I have already bought our farm farther along—bought it from The Holland Land Company."

"Just where is it?" asked Mr. Castleton.

"Well, at the place where that canal is going

[96]

to be cut through the mountain ridge, there is a big hill, of course, where there will have to be locks for taking the boats up and down. Lockport, I believe that place has been named. I figured that that locality would be a good place to live, for a big town may grow up there. Probably there will be a good market for crops and maybe good schools before long. So I have bought a few miles to the east of that point."

"I guess you are right," said Mr. Castleton. "Boats will be going in the canal as far as that within a year or two."

"Here is a map showing the location," said Mr. Armstrong. He took from his pocket a little chart and showed it to Mr. Castleton.

"I think you have made a good choice," said Mr. Castleton.

"You have made a good selection here, too," said Mr. Armstrong. "Queer what makes this ridge, though, isn't it?"

"I'll tell you what I have figured out," said Mr. Castleton. "You know Lake Ontario is only about ten miles to the north, all along here; and that mountain ridge you spoke of is two or three miles to the south, all the way along. It looks to me that the lake once went clear up to the mountain and covered all this land. Maybe it was a million years ago. But if that wasn't

the way of it, why is the ground all sandy here?
And why is this ridge here?"

Kanah was listening all this time. "I know
what it was," he said eagerly. "Maybe it was a
sand-bar in the lake."

"That is just what I think," said Mr. Castleton, "and it is mighty fine for us settlers, for
the ridge makes a very good road. It was an
Indian trail when the first white men came
through here. Never stays muddy. Rain sinks
right in or runs off."

With pleasant talk the evening passed. The
next morning, after thanking their new friends
and saying good-by, the Armstrong family

Arrival

started on. The third day after that, Father said, "We must be almost to the road leading up that big hill."

He took out his little map and examined it. "It is along there somewhere," he said.

Kanah and Patty ran on ahead. After another half mile they could be seen waving their hands.

"Here it is," Patty shouted.

"Is this it?" asked Kanah.

"It looks to me like it," said Father.

They turned south and, after going about two miles, came to the foot of the hill and started up along a winding road. It was hard work for the oxen. In places Buck and Brindle could scarcely pull the wagon. They all got out and walked, so as to lighten the load as much as possible.

Finally they were at the top, then came another few miles along a forest road. At last, in the late afternoon, they reached the spot to which they had been going all this time, and they came to rest beside a narrow road in the midst of a great forest.

"Here we are at last," said Father. "Everybody out."

"Hurrah!" shouted Kanah.

Patty danced up and down to show her joy. Even little Mary Ann clapped her hands. But

[100]

when Mother looked around and saw the dense woods on every side, her heart sank.

"Was it for this we left our good home?" she thought.

But did she say it? What she said was, "If you and Patty will pick up some dry sticks for a fire and you will light it, Kanah, I'll get our supper right away."

It was nearly the middle of May. The evening was warm. They ate their first meal there, with frogs singing in the ponds and owls hooting in the woods around them.

CHAPTER XIII

CLEARING LAND

SO here they were at last, in the place to which they had been looking forward during all that long tiresome trip. What was there here, that they should have struggled so to reach it?

There was no house to live in, no barn for the cattle. There were no smooth, cleared fields for grain or for meadow, for orchard or garden. There was nothing but trees and underbrush, trees and underbrush.

"Thank fortune there is good water," said Mother, for it turned out that the little brook that went babbling along, a few rods away, was fed by a spring, so there would be no need to dig a well.

Patty was awakened the next morning by a loud sound—*whack! whack! whack!* every few seconds.

Kanah was awakened by the same sound.

"What makes it?" asked Patty.

"Father is chopping down a tree," Mother replied.

She was trying to start a fire with flint and steel but she couldn't make the tinder catch.

"Let me try," said Kanah. It took a long time, for the sparks kept flying off without lighting the tinder, but finally he succeeded in doing it and in starting the fire for breakfast.

"Now I need some water," said Mother. "One of you run to the brook and get some."

"I'll do that," said Patty.

Mother soon had the corn mush cooking. In the cold misty morning the fire felt good. The wagon, with their household goods, stood near by; the oxen and the cow had been tethered not far away and were browsing on the low bushes.

By the time the corn mush was cooked and the breakfast ready, Father called to them that the tree was about to fall and they might come and watch it. So, leaving little Mary Ann sleeping in the wagon, the three of them went to the place where their log house was to stand and where Father had chopped the trunk of a big tree almost through.

"Don't come any nearer," he called to them, when they were still a few rods away.

He took the last few strokes of the axe, and the

[103]

great tree began to fall. He had planned for it to fall over the road, for that was the only clear space for it to go. It did go that way, but even then it caught the branches of other trees as it fell and went crashing to the ground with a tremendous noise.

"There is our first giant conquered," said Father, as he came over to them.

"See all the giants there are to conquer," said Patty, giving her arm a sweep in every direction.

"It looks like a heap of work for one pair of arms," said Mother.

"It would be fine if Kanah were a few years older, so he could help me," said Father.

They kept on talking as they sat on a log and ate their breakfast.

"Will we have any neighbors?" asked Patty.

"Well, I guess not so very near," admitted Father. "The man at the land office where I bought the place said there was a settler named Williams about a mile away, but he is on another road. I don't know in which direction."

"It will seem queer not to have any girl to play with," said Patty. Then she added, "But if I can't have Jane Marvin, maybe I don't want any one."

After Father had gone back to work, Mother could not help thinking of the pleasant house they had left, with good neighbors near by, a

[104]

church in the village and a school where Kanah and Patty could go.

After a tree had fallen, there was still much work to be done on it before it was ready for the log house that was to be built. The branches had to be chopped off; and some of them were very large. After they had been dragged away, the trunk had to be chopped into lengths for the logs.

"It is fortunate that there happen to be some hemlocks here," said Father. "They will make good logs for the house. But I have to chop all the other trees down, too, to make a space for it."

It was the time of the blooming of spring wild flowers in the woods.

"There are just thousands of them," said Patty. "I'm not sure but there are millions."

"Don't go out of sight of the wagon to pick them," said Mother. "No one knows what wild animals are roaming around here."

"Are there wild animals here?" asked Kanah that night at supper-time.

"I have been told there are some," said Father. "I suppose there are plenty of foxes and deer and woodchucks and rabbits. You remember Tom Marvin said there are some bears and wolves left. You and Patty must not go far off into the woods alone."

Day after day the swinging of Father's axe and the flying of chips went on. Every little while there was the crash of a falling tree.

"Can't I help?" asked Kanah, on the very first day.

"Yes, you may lop off some of the small limbs with your axe," Father replied.

When the limbs had been lopped off and the huge trunk of the tree had been chopped into logs, Father would put a log-chain around a log, hitch the oxen to it and they would drag it to the top of the little knoll where the house was to stand.

"I wish I could help build the new house," said Patty, about the second day.

"Well, perhaps you may," said Father. "You might drag the smaller limbs and the brush to the burning pile. And you may pick up some of the chips and put them in a pile for use in the fireplace."

"I don't know how I am to manage when it comes time to begin the actual building of the cabin," he continued. "Seems as if I can't build it all alone. And you children can't help on the heavy lifting."

"Maybe Mr. Williams would come and help you," said Patty.

"Maybe he would," said Father, "but I don't like to go and ask him, for he probably is very busy getting out stumps and putting in his crops."

"Well, I certainly shall be glad when it is built," said Mother. "It seems as if even a log house would look good to me, now that we have been so long without any."

In the middle of the afternoon, the next day, a man appeared at the edge of the clearing Father had made.

"Howdy do?" said the man. "I heard the sound of your axe and thought I'd come over and see if you had plenty of help to build your cabin."

"Thank you," said Mr. Armstrong. "That is very kind. I am the only man in our family, so I don't know just how I am going to manage."

"I'll come over and help you," said the man. "My name is Williams. I live a mile away through the woods."

"Ours is Armstrong," said Father. "We just came from Vermont."

"I am from Massachusetts," said Mr. Williams. "Came last summer. It looks to me that you have about enough logs cut. Suppose I come over the day after tomorrow to help you lay up the cabin?"

"That will be splendid," said Father. "I'll try to have everything ready."

"Isn't that neighborly?" said Mother, after Mr. Williams had gone.

"That is because this is a new country," said Father. "All the folks help each other. We'll have a chance some time."

CHAPTER XIV

THE LOG CABIN

WHEN Patty wakened, the second morning after that, her first thought was, "Oh, goody! This is the day the log house is to be started."

Both she and Kanah were through with their breakfast and had gone over to the place where the logs were piled, even before Mr. Williams came. When he did come, he brought another man with him.

"This is Mr. Towner, the neighbor who lives beyond me," he said. "He has come to help, too."

"That is good of you folks," said Father. "Only the day before yesterday I was wondering how I was to build this house all alone; and now here are two new neighbors come to help me."

The three men began to lay the logs up, one on top of another, for the four walls. They fitted the notched ends at the corners. Patty and Kanah were now here, now there, watching the men lift the logs and fit the corners. Gradually the walls grew higher and higher. Patty wondered how long it would take them to build it.

"Can you do it in one day?" she asked.

The Log House

"No, not in one day," Father replied. "But we ought to do it in two or three days."

When the sides were high enough, they placed shorter and shorter logs at the two ends to form a peak for the roof. At the very top they placed the ridge pole.

[110]

"Aren't we going to have any window?" asked Patty.

"Oh, yes; we'll saw places for two windows," said Mr. Williams. "You won't be able to buy any glass for them here, but you can use oiled paper."

"Aren't we going to have any door?" asked Kanah.

"Yes; we are going to saw a place for a door, too," said Father.

"Are we going to have a fireplace?" asked Patty.

"Yes; we'll build a fireplace at one end," Mr. Williams replied.

"I wish we could help," said Patty.

"Well, now, there is one thing you and Kanah could do," said Father. "Wherever there is a chink between the logs, you can stuff chips and wedges of wood in to fill up the space. You can hunt up some moss, too, and stuff it in the smaller chinks. Then, when I get time, I'll put mud in them and we'll have walls that won't let the wind through."

By the third day, the house was ready for the roof; and the men split many long shingles and fastened them up on the roof poles. Then they started to build the fireplace.

Now, it happened in that place that there were many stones lying here and there.

"If these youngsters want to help, they might bring the smaller stones that are lying around and pile them handy," said Mr. Williams. "We men can bring big ones on the stone-boat and you can have a fine stone chimney."

"That is a good idea," said Father, "but what am I to do for bricks for the oven? We can't use stones for that."

Kanah and Patty were already bringing whatever stones they could lift. Even little Mary Ann began to fetch tiny stones, thinking it a fine game.

Patty heard Mr. Williams say, "I have some bricks left from making my oven. If only we can get them over here, you are welcome to them. There is a new brick-kiln about ten miles away, but it would take a lot of time to go there and back. You are welcome to mine."

"That is very kind," said Father, "I'll go right away."

He hitched the oxen to the stone-boat and went through the woods for the bricks. The stone-boat was not really a boat at all, but merely a platform of heavy planks about eight feet long and three feet wide, with the front slanting upward so that it could be drawn over rough ground. It was so low that stones could easily be rolled onto it.

When the bricks had been brought and the

oven was done, Patty asked, "What are we going to do for beds?"

But the men had planned that. They built beds against the walls, and they laid planks on the crosspieces over their heads for a loft for Kanah to sleep in.

"What are we going to do for chairs?" asked Kanah, who knew they had brought only one with them.

"Here are your chairs," said Mr. Williams. He brought some blocks of wood in and stood them up on the ground.

"What are we going to do for a table to eat on?" asked Patty.

"Watch us make one," Father replied.

He and Mr. Williams split off a wide plank from the side of a log. They placed it on blocks of wood of the right height. And there was a long narrow table.

"And what else do you children want made?" asked Mr. Williams, smiling at them as if it were a joke and hinting that he and Father could make anything they could ask for.

"What are we going to do for a floor?" asked Kanah.

"We'll have to do without a floor for the present," said Father. "We can't expect our kind neighbors to spend any more time to help us, for they must go home and plant their crops, but I'll put in a floor as soon as I can manage."

Then Patty thought of another question. "What are we going to do for a door? You haven't put any door in the doorway."

"We can't take time to make one now," said Father. "After a while I'll make a door, but meanwhile maybe Mother will hang a quilt up there."

Mother did hang a quilt up for a door.

Kanah and Patty did not shout the good news that they had a house, though they felt like doing so, but they showed their joy in a better way, by helping to bring the things from the wagon and place them in the cabin.

There was already a good fire burning in the new fireplace, where Mother had hung a kettle and boiled some potatoes. With those and some hot biscuits, some doughnuts and Vermont maple syrup, she had a good supper waiting for the hungry men when they all sat down together to the first meal in the new house.

Both Mr. and Mrs. Armstrong and Kanah and Patty thanked the two neighbors who had helped them build it.

"If ever you need some help, I'll come over and give you a hand," said Mr. Armstrong. "And our latchstring will always be out for you."

CHAPTER XV

BRIGHT PEWTER

"I DO wish our pewter dishes could be polished," said Mother one day. "They have become so dark and dull that it is no pleasure to look at them any more."

"I'll brighten them," said Patty. "What shall I scour them with?"

"That is what I don't know," Mother replied. "Back at our old home there were those scouring rushes that grew down by the bog, but maybe there are none of those growing in these woods."

"Oh, yes, there are," said Kanah, eagerly. "Do you remember the day Molly wandered off? Well, there were some of those scouring rushes near the place where I found her—lots of them."

"Are you sure they are the same?" Mother inquired. "Are they round and do they have joints every two or three inches?"

"Yes," said Kanah. "And they are rough to the touch."

"I wish I had some," said Mother.

"I'll go and get them," said Kanah, and he started to the door, ready to go at once.

"I'll go, too," said Patty, and she started to the door.

"Oh, I would rather get along with dull pewter than to have you children go far off into the woods," said Mother. "You might get lost, or some wild animal might come after you. You had better not go."

An hour later, when Patty and Kanah were pulling weeds in the corn patch, Patty said, "Wouldn't it be nice if we could get some of those rushes for Mother?"

"I don't see what difference it makes if the pewter is dull," said Kanah. "It is just as good to eat from."

"But, Kanah, it doesn't shine any more. Our cabin is dark inside anyway, and there are many things that are not as nice as they were in our old home. I think it would be lovely if the pewter were bright and shiny."

"We'll go and get some of those rushes," said Kanah. "Mother did not forbid us. Come on."

"Could you find them again?" asked Patty.

"Of course," he replied. "I know just where they were—in a boggy sort of place beside a little pond, off in that direction." He pointed to the woods.

"Let's get them and s'prise Mother," said Patty.

"All right," Kanah agreed.

They started off into the woods, but had not gone far when Patty said, "How are we to find the way back?"

Kanah considered a moment. "Why, we'll come back by the sun," he said. "We are going right away from it now. When we come back, we must go toward it."

"Can we see it in the deep forest?" asked Patty.

"Not so well as here," said Kanah, "but if we look sharp we can find it through the tree-tops."

"I think this is the way to go," he said.

They walked through the woods, kicking up the old dry leaves, going among wild flowers and bushes, over logs and around stumps. After going in that direction for several minutes, Kanah stopped and looked around.

"This doesn't look like the right way," he said. "I believe I went the other way." So they changed their path.

But when they had gone in that direction for some time, and had not yet found the rushes, he said, "I wonder where it was that I saw them."

"Don't you know, Kanah?" asked Patty, in alarm.

"I almost know," he said. "There were tall

hickory trees near them and a big patch of white lilies. It was a sort of boggy place."

"We'd better go back," said Patty.

"Oh, shucks, I'll find them," said Kanah. "If you are afraid, you can go back now."

"I am not afraid," declared Patty. "I'll go as far as you will, any day."

They went on, in and out among the trees, in and out among wild flowers. They saw plenty of lilies and bishop's caps, but no rushes, with stems of green and white.

"I don't believe you saw any rushes," said Patty, when they had been hunting for a long time.

"I did truly see some," said Kanah. "There were a lot of them, too."

Then, in a moment they had to run to get away from that place, for a rattlesnake appeared in their path.

"If ever you see a rattlesnake," Mother had often said, "just get away as fast as you can run."

They had no more than stopped running before Patty said, "Oh, Kanah, see that animal over there."

"Where?" he asked.

"Off there among the trees." She pointed to a place a few rods away, where some creature could be seen moving in the underbrush.

"It's a deer!" exclaimed Kanah.

"Oh—oh—h!" said Patty. "Two of them!"

"Three!" exclaimed Kanah. "See the tiny one."

The deer must have heard them, for they bounded swiftly away through the underbrush and out of sight.

"I wonder whether there are other animals in this part of the woods," said Patty, "and do you s'pose there might be some Indians?"

"I wonder," said Kanah.

They kept on a few rods farther. Then Kanah shouted, "Here they are! Here are the scouring rushes."

Both stooped to pick them. They were about as big around as one's little finger and felt rough, so they were not pleasant to hold. In spite of that, Kanah and Patty each picked a large handful.

"Won't it be a nice s'prise for Mother?" said Patty.

"Now we'll go back," said Kanah.

They started back along the trail they thought they had come, but had not gone very far when Kanah said, "This isn't the way we came. See, we didn't pass this pond."

"No, we didn't," agreed Patty. "We had better look at the sun."

But there was no sun to be seen and no rays of sunlight filtering through the tree-tops.

"It must be under a cloud," said Kanah. "We'll wait till it comes out again."

But it did not come out from under the cloud, for, while they had been picking the rushes, clouds had covered all the sky.

Lost:

"How shall we ever get home?" said Patty, anxiously.

"Don't cry," begged Kanah. "We'll get home sometime."

"I am not crying, Kanah Armstrong, but you

know yourself we can never find the way if we can't see the sun. And what are we going to do?"

"Let's shout," said Kanah. He called out, "Too—whoo—oo—oo!"

—the Deer

But there was no answer—no sound at all except the croaking of frogs in the ponds and the twittering of birds in the trees.

Then Patty called, in her high clear voice, "Too—whoo—oo—oo!"

Still there was no answer.

"We are lost," said Patty.

"We had better just stay right here till the sun comes out again," said Kanah. "Maybe Father will come to hunt for us."

Soon the storm was upon them, the wind sweeping through the tree-tops and the rain descending on them.

At that very moment Father went into the house to be out of the storm.

"Where are Kanah and Patty?" asked Mother.

"Kanah and Patty? Aren't they here all safe? I thought they must have come to the house, when I saw they were not weeding the corn."

"No; they haven't been here," said Mother. "I hope they didn't go after scouring rushes."

"I'll go and hunt for them," said Father.

He put on his heavy coat and went out into the storm.

"I wish I knew which way to go," he thought, as he started into the forest.

Every little while he shouted at the top of his voice, "Kanah! Patty!"

Now, it happened that he went in exactly the opposite direction from that which the children had taken, so they did not hear his shouts. He went on and on.

After half an hour the storm stopped as suddenly as it had begun. The sun shone again.

The trees glistened with raindrops. Kanah searched the sky, until he found the sun, shining through the trees here and there.

"Come, Patty, this is the way," he said.

Back along the forest paths they went, clutching the scouring rushes in their hands; and they came to the clearing just as Father, having made up his mind that he must go in some other direction, came out of the forest at the other edge of the clearing.

"Here are some scouring rushes," shouted Kanah and Patty together, as they came into the log house.

Then they stopped suddenly. "Why, Mother, what are you crying for?" Patty asked.

"Oh! I thought you were lost in the woods," said Mother.

"We were," said Patty.

"But we found our way out," said Kanah.

Mother had Patty in her arms and was saying to the two of them, "You must never go off into the forest again, for scouring rushes or anything else."

Father, who had come in just then, said, "Don't forbid them ever to go. Pioneers, both old and young, have to learn how to look out for themselves amid dangers. But they had better not go into the deep forest again, unless the sun is shining bright."

Mother took the rushes and broke them into pieces a few inches long and rubbed them back and forth over the pewter dishes. When one bunch was all broken up, she took fresh ones. Patty and Kanah helped, too. When they were through, there were the pewter dishes as shiny and bright as though they were made of silver.

"There, now, I feel more civilized," said Mother. "No good housekeeper lets her pewter ware stay dull, even if she does have to live in a log house in the woods."

CHAPTER XVI

THE SALT LICK

THE pioneers who settled in the great forests and made themselves homes in the clearings had many hardships to put up with; and the Armstrong family had their share. As spring passed and summer came, vast numbers of mosquitoes came out of the forest and the swampy places.

"There must be millions of them," said Patty, as she swung her arms to shoo them away.

"Yes, there are millions of them, I guess," said Mother, with a sigh. "There is another thing that is bothering me, too. What are we to do for salt? Our salt bag is empty."

"What is that? The salt gone? I was just going to take some out for the cattle," said Father. "They are in need of salt, too."

"See how little there is," said Mother. She shook the bag to get every particle of it out.

"We can't eat food without salt," she added.

"Well, I suppose I'll just have to stop clearing the land and go to get some," said Father. "I might as well go to-day as to put it off till to-morrow."

"Where will you get it?" asked Patty. "Is there a store near here?"

She had often gone to the village store in Vermont and bought salt.

"Well, I suppose I might get some by going to the settlement at Lockport," said Father, "but I would have to pay out money for it there and we must keep what we have till some crops are ready to bring us more. I'll go down to the salt licks to get some."

"What is a salt lick?" asked Patty. She involuntarily stuck out her tongue, as if she were ready to lick some up when she found it.

"Don't you know that?" asked Kanah, who was starting with a bucket to get some water from the spring. "Ten years old and you don't know what a salt lick is," he taunted her.

"Smarty! Maybe you don't know yourself," said Patty.

"Indeed I do. It is a place where there is salt found on the ground, and wild animals go there to lick it up, when they are hungry for salt."

"Very well said," remarked Father.

"Do you mean it is right on the ground?"

asked Patty, who could not believe such an un-
usual thing.

"Yes, in some places," replied Father. "You
know the deer and the foxes and other animals
have to have salt to eat, as well as folks. However, in the place I am going for it, I won't have
to scrape it up from the ground. It is made there
so folks can come to buy it."

"May I go with you?" asked Patty.

"Why, yes, I don't see any harm in it. What
do you say, Mother?" He turned to Mrs. Armstrong for an answer.

"If you think it is safe," she replied.

"And can I go?" asked Kanah, eagerly.

"Well, now, that is different," said Father.
"Mother can't be left here alone, she and Mary
Ann, without any man around. I guess you'll
have to stay here, Kanah."

"Oh, pshaw!" said Kanah. But he stood a
little straighter to think Father would trust him
with a man's job.

"I think I could manage alone," said Mother.

"No; I won't consider that for a moment,"
said Father. "Kanah must stay this time.
Maybe in another year he can go off on such
trips all by himself. Or maybe we'll have
neighbors by that time. But with the nearest
neighbor a mile away, Mother and Mary Ann

shall not be left alone. Some wild animal might come prowling around."

At this Patty looked startled. Mother was so sweet and so frail looking, what would she do if a wild animal did come?

As if he read her thought, Father said, "Kanah knows how to use a gun. I am going to leave one of the guns here by the door."

"How far is it to the salt licks?" asked Mother.

"Oh, about five miles," said Father, "but the road is not very good. In fact it is hardly more than a trail through the forest part of the way. So it will take us quite a time."

"We'll be all right—Kanah and I and Mary Ann," said Mother bravely.

Then Father seemed to forget about the salt, for he said to Kanah, "Come and help me load on a cord of wood."

Patty followed them across the clearing, where a large pile of wood had been cut into the proper lengths. She watched the two of them carry it to the wagon and pile it on neatly.

"Why do we take the wood along?" she asked. "I thought we were going for salt."

"So we are," answered Father. "This is our money. The man who has the salt will give us some of it for cordwood. He has more salt than he needs. We have more wood than we need. We'll trade."

"Oh," said Patty. "It is queer money, though."

"Patty! Patty!" called Mother from the doorway of the log house. "Come in and put on your pink calico dress. You should dress up a bit when you go away."

Patty ran into the house and in a few minutes appeared, all fresh and clean, with her pink dress on and her brown curls hanging in ringlets down her neck.

Father looked at her in satisfaction as he thought, "Well, if we do live in the wilderness, there aren't many city girls that could outshine my Patty."

The wood was finally loaded; the oxen had been yoked and hitched to the wagon; and they were ready to go. Father lifted Patty up to the seat in front. She might easily have climbed up, but didn't want to get her fresh dress dirty.

"We'll be back before dark," said Father, as they drove away.

The patient oxen walked slowly along the rough forest road, where the trees met over their heads like the arches of a beautiful church. Slow going it was till they came to a turnpike, when Patty gave four cents to the tollgate keeper as they passed. Finally they reached the place where they were to get the precious salt. "Salt works," Father called the place.

Patty looked with interest at the huge kettles filled with water, in some of which all the water had boiled away, so that nothing remained but the white salt.

"Are you a new settler?" asked the man who came to wait on them.

"Yes," replied Mr. Armstrong. "We came from Vermont only this spring. Brought some salt with us but it is all gone."

"Can't get along without salt," said the man. "How much do you want?"

"As much as I can get for that wood," replied Mr. Armstrong, pointing to his wagon.

"I give a bushel of salt for a cord of wood," said the man. "Here, Henry," he called to another man, who was busy at the other side of the works. "Help Mr. Armstrong unload his wood."

The two unloaded the wood and piled it neatly.

"Now give him a bushel of salt," said the owner.

"I suppose it was discovered that there was salt here because wild animals used it for a salt lick," said Father.

"They come here still," said the man. "Oh, yes, the first settlers noticed it. Why, the deer would come here from miles and miles away and gather around this hollow and lick up the salt. We figured that if there was salt on the top of the ground, there must be some of it under the ground and we dug a well. Sure enough, the water was salty. And we've been making salt here ever since."

It was five o'clock before they started back. The sun was still high, but in the forest it had begun to grow dark. The slow oxen plodded their way along. When they had gone more than half way home the oxen suddenly stopped.

"What can be the trouble?" exclaimed Father.

"Maybe there is a wild animal around," said Patty, half fearing that there was one, half hoping that there was one, so that she could brag of it to Kanah.

She peered off through the forest. There was a dark form ambling along, a few rods away.

"See, Father, there is a wild animal," she said. "It is as big as a bear."

Father looked eagerly in the direction in which she pointed, but Patty first made out what it was.

"It *is* a bear!" she whispered. "Oh, dear, he may come after us."

Father climbed out of the wagon. "You stay

[131]

right there on the seat," said he. "I won't let anything happen to you."

He started for the bear, with his gun in his hand. Patty tried to be brave, but it wasn't easy to sit there, with Father going farther and farther away.

The Bear

"Bang!" went the gun.

But before Father could load it again, the bear had traveled off through the wood and was lost to sight among the underbrush.

"Don't go after it," pleaded Patty.

"No, I won't this time," said Father, "but sometime I'll come down here, when I have things all safe at home, and shoot a few of these creatures."

He climbed into the wagon and they drove on. They reached the clearing just as darkness settled down.

"Hello!" shouted Kanah, who was watching for them.

"How is everything, son?" asked Father.

"All safe," Kanah replied. "All safe now, but we've had an adventure."

"An adventure right here at home?" asked Father. "What happened?"

"A wolf came and stuck his head in the door."

"A wolf!" exclaimed Father. "Are you sure you are not mistaken?"

Mother had come out of the house, with little Mary Ann. "No, he is not mistaken," she said. "I saw the wolf with my own eyes. He just pushed the quilt aside and poked his head inside. Oh, but I was scared!"

"What did you do? How did you drive him away?" asked Father; for since they were all safe, he decided they must have scared the wolf somehow.

"Mother threw the fire-shovel at him," said Kanah.

"Next I threw the tongs at him and they hit him in the head," said Mother.

"We both threw things as fast as we could,"

[133]

said Kanah. "And then I got the gun and fired it after him."

"But you didn't hit him, did you?" asked Patty.

"No; I missed," he acknowledged. "But he went off into the woods."

"He might come back to-night," said Father. "I'll stay awake and be ready for him, with my gun. And I'll make that door for our house to-morrow."

"Why, Mother, you are all a-tremble," said Patty.

"I'll be all right soon, dear. What a splendid lot of salt you have!"

CHAPTER XVII

THE WOLF

TIRED as Mr. Armstrong was with the hard work he had done that forenoon and the long drive in the afternoon to the salt works, he did not go to bed that night, till long after midnight. There was a good reason.

"I'll stay here by the door and watch," he said. "By to-morrow night, we'll have a strong wooden door here that can be banged shut in case of danger."

He placed both guns on the floor within reach.

"Let me watch, too," begged Kanah.

"Well, I suppose you are getting big enough to do such things," said Father. "Yes, you may stay up with me. If that wolf comes prowling around, maybe you can use one of the guns."

He arranged the quilt that hung at the door so there was a crack for looking out.

At first Kanah was so wide awake with the excitement of it that he had no desire to go to sleep, but as the hours passed, he grew drowsy and could hardly keep his eyes open.

"You might as well lean against the table and take a nap," said Father. "I'll call you if any wild animal comes."

Kanah was glad to catch a few winks of sleep. He thought they were only a few winks, but it was after two o'clock when he was wakened by the howling of a wolf in the forest. He had heard this sound many times, but never so near as this.

They waited in silence for several minutes. Then Father leaned forward and peered through the crack between the quilt and the door jamb. Kanah tried to look out, too.

"Hush!" said Father.

They kept very still. Soon a shadowy form appeared at the edge of the clearing. Closer and closer it came.

"Take this gun," said Father, handing one of them to Kanah. "You keep close by me and don't fire till I tell you to."

They waited till the animal was plainly in view in the moonlight.

"Now," said Father.

The two guns went off at the same time, with a loud bang.

"Mercy me!" said Mother, wakened by the sound. "What is the matter?"

"The wolf," said Kanah. "Keep back!"

There was, however, no need for caution. The animal did not stir.

"You stay here till I call you," said Father to Kanah.

He went quickly out to the dark form and found it stretched on the ground.

The Wolf

"Come on, Kanah," Father called.

Mother came to the door of the cabin. "Did you kill him?" she asked.

"He is as dead as a door-nail," Father replied, "and I'll get a bounty for killing him—a bounty from the State, in addition to ridding this neighborhood of a savage beast."

[137]

The next morning, Father asked, "Do any of you know where those nails are that I brought along with us? I need them for making the door."

"Why, I haven't seen those nails, not ever since we came here," Mother said. "But I remember them—big nails that the blacksmith forged for you. I'll hunt for them."

"Where are you going to get the boards for the door?" asked Kanah.

"Won't use boards," Father replied. "The nearest sawmill is so far away that it would take all day to go there and back. I'll hew out some planks from one of those big logs."

"I'll find the nails while you are hewing the planks," said Mother. "They are sure to be here somewhere, but there are not many of them."

There were many logs lying about, from which Mr. Armstrong could make planks for the door. He chose a large one of white oak, a straight splendid piece of the trunk of a tree. First he had to split a piece off from one side with the axe, and that took many hard strokes. Then, when the first plank was split off, he had to smooth it with the axe. That was a hard job. Then he split off a second plank and then a third one.

"I found the nails," said Mother, when he

came into the house for dinner. "Good long stout nails they are, too."

"They will need to be long and stout," said Father. "These planks are nearly three inches thick."

After dinner he hewed out two shorter planks for crosspieces at the top and bottom. When he had nailed them all together, there was a heavy strong door for their log house.

"This door is strong enough to keep an elephant out," declared Kanah.

"Oh, are there elephants in these woods?" asked Patty, with wide-open eyes. Having seen a bear and a wolf in one day, she was ready to believe almost anything.

"Oh, Patty, don't you know that there aren't any elephants in all America?" Kanah laughed at her.

"Of course I know," said Patty, tossing her head. "Elephants live in Asia and Africa."

She was reciting her geography lesson now. "I guess I know where elephants and lions and tigers live, but these woods are so big that almost anything might live in them."

Kanah helped to carry the heavy door to the house and stand it up.

"Where are the big hinges I brought along?" asked Father.

"I found those, too, when I was looking for the nails," Mother answered.

She brought out two large iron hinges, wrought by hand, which had been on their front door once upon a time.

"It will seem like home to have these hinges on our front door here," she said.

Finally the hinges were fastened on and the door could swing open and shut. Patty fairly danced with glee.

"A door! A real door!" she exclaimed. "My, but that is nice."

There was still the latch to put on. Father made a bar of heavy strong wood, which he placed on the door to slip into a slot of wood on the casing.

"There, that is a good safe latch," he said.

"But how are we going to get in, if we are out-side?" asked Patty.

"Just watch," said Father.

He bored a hole in the bar of wood and another one in the door, about a foot above it. Then he tied one end of a string through the hole in the bar and put the other end through the hole in the door, so that it hung outside.

"I see how it works," said Kanah. "A person outside will pull the string and that will lift the latch."

"Exactly," said Father.

"And if we want to feel safe inside, we can pull the latch-string in," said Patty.

"That is it," said Kanah.

"No creature will push that door open," said Father.

"And now with salt in the house and the wolf killed and a strong door on our house, I'll go back to clearing the land to-morrow."

CHAPTER XVIII

MAKING PEGS

"WHAT are you doing, Kanah?" asked Patty one day, not long after the wolf was killed.

"Haven't you eyes to see with?" he asked, teasingly.

Indeed Patty had sharp eyes and they were wide open now in wonderment. In his two hands he was holding the big beetle, a heavy wooden tool something like a croquet mallet, only eight or ten times as large, with iron bands around the ends of the mallet part to keep the wood from splitting when it was pounded down on something. In front of him, resting on two blocks of wood, was a flat square plate of iron in which were round holes of different sizes.

Through one of these holes Kanah was trying to drive a square piece of wood by hitting it with the beetle.

"Why, Kanah, are you trying to drive that square piece of wood into that round hole?" she asked. "That isn't sense. You can never do it."

"Can, too," he declared. "Just see me do it."

He raised the beetle above the stick and

brought it down with a tremendous whack, which drove the stick through and cut off the edges of it, making it a round smooth piece of wood a half-inch thick and about four inches long.

"Oh, you did do it," acknowledged Patty. "What is it for?"

"What does it look like?" asked Kanah.

"It looks like a peg," said Patty, promptly.

"That's what it is," said Kanah.

On the ground near him was a pile of those little sticks of wood, which Father had sharpened at one end. Kanah took up one of these sticks, which were rough and slivery and square, placed the sharpened end in one of the holes, gave it a few whacks with the beetle, and there was a second peg.

"What are you going to do with them?" asked Patty.

"Father and I are going to put a floor down in the log house," he answered, as he took up another stick of wood and slipped it into the hole.

"Why, Kanah, you can't lay a floor," protested Patty. "You aren't big enough."

"I can help. I'm making the pegs for fastening the boards down to the crosspieces," he replied.

Before he had made many more pegs, his arm ached with lifting that heavy beetle.

"Let me make one," begged Patty, after she had watched him make a dozen.

Kanah wasn't sorry to rest his arm, so he said, "Try if you want to, but you never can."

She placed a stick in one of the holes, but found she couldn't lift the big beetle very far from the ground, for it weighed about ten pounds. Patty was one who never gave up a thing if she could possibly do it, so she kept on trying; but she finally had to admit that she couldn't.

"I knew you couldn't," said Kanah. "Girls can make samplers and sew carpet rags and piece quilts and wash dishes and do such things, but they can't do much of anything worth while."

Patty was indignant. "I can, too, Kanah Armstrong. I can run as fast as you can and climb trees and make candles—and that is worth while—and I can learn my Bible verses quicker and I can— I can—" She tried to think of some big splendid thing she could do.

Then she ended with, "You just wait. Sometime I'll s'prise you. You'll just see what I can do."

Kanah was to see that promise fulfilled before the next winter was over.

He went back to making pegs, but his arms were soon tired and he was glad when Father came along on his way to the house, after chopping down trees all the afternoon, and said,

"Want to rest a while, son? I'll try my hand at it."

Father's strong arms lifted the beetle and brought it down with such force on the wood that it was astonishing to Kanah and Patty how quickly he pounded pegs through, one after another.

"How are you going to drive these pegs through the thick floor boards?" asked Patty. She knew they couldn't be driven, like an iron nail, by pounding them into the board.

"I have an auger just this size," Father replied. "I'll bore a hole with the auger and then drive the peg into it."

"I knew that," bragged Kanah.

"We'll need a lot of these pegs," said Father. "You keep on making them every time you get a chance, Kanah. Then they'll be ready when we need them."

Every few days after that, Kanah could be seen making pegs for the floor.

"I'll surely be glad when that new floor is in," said Mother.

CHAPTER XIX

A VISITOR

SUMMER had passed, with the little clearing growing larger each week, as Mr. Armstrong kept chopping down the trees. The corn he had planted in patches among the stumps had grown taller than any corn he had ever seen before and had been full of big yellow ears. There were piles of huge yellow pumpkins here and there. The beans had been pulled and the turnips and potatoes had been dug, so there was plenty of food for the winter.

One day in October when the leaves had turned and the woods were a glory of scarlet and gold, Kanah was shooting at a hickory tree with his gun, trying to hit a certain spot, when Patty came over to watch him.

"I wish we could have brought along the bow and arrow you gave me, Kanah," she said. "I'd like to learn to shoot straight."

"I'll make you another one," he offered.

He went into the woods and found a piece of ash wood, and day after day, as he had time, he whittled it with his jackknife. After a few days it began to look like a real bow. As he was working on it one day, Patty came out to the stump on which he was sitting, bringing a basin of hot doughnuts which Mother had just made.

"Whew! Those are good," said Kanah, as he finished the first one. "I'll bet there isn't anybody this side of the Atlantic Ocean who can make better doughnuts than Mother."

"I'm sure there isn't," agreed Patty.

They were at the far side of the clearing. As Father had gone through the woods to help Mr. Williams with a log-rolling, they were alone that day.

Suddenly Patty's eyes caught sight of some one moving among the trees at a little distance. Before she could say a word of warning to Kanah, there was a young Indian coming toward them.

"Oh, dear! Oh!" thought Patty. "What shall we do?"

Her feet seemed glued to the ground, as he came walking quietly toward them. She whispered to Kanah, but not a word did either of them speak aloud, as the Indian stood in front of them, not six feet away.

Patty noticed the knife in his belt. She

noticed his straight black hair and his reddish brown skin. She noticed his big brown eyes. She noticed how tall and straight he stood.

She waited for him to speak, but he stood there as straight as an arrow, as silent as the new moon. Then it came to her that he was being polite.

"Good morning," she said, "have one." She held out the basin of doughnuts, still fresh and warm.

He took one. Kanah looked up and nodded, but went on with his whittling. No thanks did the Indian speak, but quickly ate the delicious doughnut.

"He doesn't act so dreadfully fierce," thought Patty. "Maybe if I give him some more doughnuts, he won't harm us."

With that, she offered the basin again. And he took the two that were left.

"Good! Good!" he grunted, after the third one had disappeared.

For a few moments, he watched Kanah whittle. Then he suddenly leaned over and pulled the half-finished bow away from him.

Kanah stood up and said, "No; it is for my sister," and he pointed to Patty.

The Indian held up the bow. "No good," he said.

He took his knife from his belt and began to

whittle it. Kanah and Patty stood looking on, afraid to go, lest they should anger him, afraid to stay, lest he should turn and harm them with his knife.

Suddenly he said again, "No good. No good."

He threw the bow down and placed the knife back in his belt.

"No good," he repeated. "I make one. I make good one. I bring."

Patty, seeing there was nothing to fear, said to him, "Where are your feathers? Where are your fringes?"

She put her hand up to her head. She put it down along her dress. He grunted, "I bring."

With that he turned and walked swiftly off into the woods. The two children stood and watched till he was out of sight, then they ran like two deer to the cabin.

"Mother, an Indian!" they exclaimed.

"An Indian? Where?" she asked.

She slammed the door shut and started to drop the wooden bar, when Kanah said, "Don't be afraid. He has gone. And he is a good one."

"I gave him some doughnuts," said Patty, "and he is coming again."

"And he is going to make a bow for Patty," said Kanah.

When they told Father that night, he said, "I

understand there are some Indians living ten or twelve miles from here. Let's hope this one doesn't make us another visit."

"Oh, but he will," said Patty. "He is going to bring me a bow and arrows."

For several days Mother glanced outdoors every once in a while, ready to shut the door and bar it if need be. She took pains to have plenty of doughnuts in the crock.

Two weeks had passed when, without any warning, there he stood at the door of the cabin. There he stood, with his Indian garments on, his feathers and his fringes and his moccasins.

"Oh! Oh!" Mother was saying, as she reached to shut the door, when she noticed in his hand a large bow and three arrows.

"For her," he said, pointing to Patty.

Oh, a beautiful bow it was, four feet long, decorated with little figures burned into the wood, smooth to the touch as a piece of glass. The Indian placed one of the arrows against the string and drew it. Away it sped, up into the sky, almost out of sight. Then it came down at the far edge of the clearing, hit a log and remained standing in it.

"Whew! That was a great shot," said Kanah. "I'll get the arrow."

The Indian placed another arrow against the string and handed the bow to Patty.

"Shoot," he said.

He showed her how to place the notch of the arrow against the string and how to hold the bow, but when she tried to bend the bow, her fingers slipped on the arrow.

"This way," said the Indian, as he hooked her

The Indian

first three fingers around the string. With her left hand pushing the bow, she let the arrow speed on its way. It did not go so far as the Indian's had gone, but far enough to make Patty feel a thrill of joy.

After she had shot several times, she let Kanah take it. He found that he was strong

[151]

enough to shoot a long way, but that he couldn't hit a mark, as the Indian could.

Soon Mother brought a bowl of doughnuts and offered them. The Indian smiled and took three. Almost before they knew it, he and Patty and Kanah were talking together. Kanah and Patty did most of the talking, but their friend would nod his head and put in a word occasionally.

"Good," he said, when Mother offered the doughnuts again and a dish of maple syrup with them.

"Much good," he said, when he had finished.

When he left, it was with the promise that he would bring a bow and arrow to Kanah the next time he came.

CHAPTER XX

THE PEDDLER

ONE day not long after this, a man was walking along a country road a few miles from Albany. He was bent over, for on his back was a heavy pack and in one hand he carried a black leather satchel.

Any one living in that part of the country would at once have known that he was the pack peddler who twice a year, in spring and in fall, traveled up and down those roads, offering his wares for sale. The housewives usually gave him a welcome, for they did not often go to the city, and so were glad of a chance to buy some of his goods.

In his pack were needles and pins, thread and buckles, ribbons and yarns of various colors, buttons, hooks and eyes, some rolls of calico and of cambric, besides cheap jewelry—rings and lockets, neck chains and collar buttons and even some silver teaspoons.

All these things he usually carried, but in addition to these, he had to-day in his satchel one thing much more costly than any of the others.

but which he felt sure some one of his customers would be glad to buy.

The day was warm, one of the Indian summer days, but there was a touch of rawness in the air, which made the peddler think the fine days might be about over and that he had better hurry to sell out his stock. Just as this thought was in his mind, he happened to glance up at the sky and saw a flock of wild geese flying over.

Soon he came to an unpainted house with a clump of evergreens in the front yard. He was sure of a welcome here, for the farmer's wife never failed to buy several things, besides giving him a good dinner. He went to the side door and knocked. In a moment it was opened by the farmer's wife, whose name was Mrs. Winters. She gave him welcome and invited him in.

He was glad to slip the pack from his back, for it was a heavy one to carry as he trudged all those miles from one house to another.

"There will be a change in the weather before long," he said. "Cold weather is coming. The wild geese are flying south."

"I began to think you weren't coming this fall," said Mrs. Winters. "What have you to-day?"

"I have needles and pins, thread and buttons, tape and edging, darning-needles, hooks and eyes, knitting-needles and a nice lot of jewelry."

[154]

Here he paused for breath and then went on, "But look for yourself."

With that he opened his pack and let her look it over.

"I'll have some thread—white thread and black thread and linen thread," she said. "I'll have some bone buttons and some pearl buttons and some knitting-needles and a paper of pins."

He took these articles out for her and then fumbled around in his pack and found some narrow black velvet ribbon.

"You'll be sure to want some of this," he said.

"No; not that," she replied. "But I would like a few yards of that pretty calico and a few of the book muslin."

He measured them and cut them off, then brought out some candle-snuffers and a box of jewelry.

"I'll take the pair of candle-snuffers," she said, "but as for the rings and the lockets, don't you know that I don't wear such gewgaws?"

So he put them back; but he felt around under the rolls of cloth in the satchel till he put his hand on a little polished wooden box.

"If only you knew what is in this box, you wouldn't call this a gewgaw," he said.

"And what is in the box?" she asked, for it made her curious to know, his saying, "if only you knew what is in the box."

He held it there for a moment, but did not offer it to her.

"Not often does one of us peddlers get hold of anything so rare as this," he said, "and for such a low price! Would you like to see it?"

"Just as you please," Mrs. Winters replied. "I might care to see it and I might not care to see it. But how am I to see it if you never open the box?"

With that he opened the box and let her see what was in it.

"Oh! What a pretty string of gold beads!" she exclaimed.

She held them up and looked at them carefully; then she fastened them on her neck and looked at herself in the looking-glass that hung on the wall.

"They seem to be quite nice ones," she said.

"Nice ones? I should say they are. Solid gold those are, solid gold, and a regular bargain, if there ever was one."

"How do you know they are solid gold?" she asked.

"Didn't I take them to the jeweler in Albany?" he said. "Didn't he tell me they were solid gold and worth fifty dollars if they are worth a cent?"

"But where did you get them? And how

much do you want for them?" she asked. "I can't pay fifty dollars."

"Who said you had to?" he protested. "I got them at a bargain from a man who bought them from a little girl who needed money badly. I'll let you have those beads for fifteen dollars," he said.

"But why didn't the jeweler buy them?" she asked.

"He didn't have the chance," the peddler replied. "I knew that one of my customers would take them. If you want them, say so; if you don't want them, say so. If you don't take them, I am sure that Mrs. Parton, down at the four corners, will be glad to buy them."

Then the farmer's wife was seized with a great desire to have the beads. She remembered that her husband had just sold his crop of wheat and had brought the money home. So when he came in to dinner, she begged him to buy them for her.

After a good dinner the pack peddler went on his way, and there were Patty's gold beads on the neck of a farmer's wife, not far from Albany.

CHAPTER XXI

NEW NEIGHBORS

IT was the middle of winter. Snow lay deep on the ground through all the woods. It covered the ground and the fallen trees, the logs and the ugly stumps with a blanket of white. The reflection from the snow outside lighted up the dark cabin, making it a much pleasanter place than in summer.

On one of these wintry days, Kanah and Patty sat at the long plank table finishing their arithmetic lesson; for, since there was no school for miles around, Mother taught them their lessons at home. On week days they studied their school books; on Sundays they learned their Bible verses.

"You are not to grow up ignorant, even if we do live in the woods," she had said.

"That is true," said Father. "Until there are enough settlers around here so we can have a schoolhouse within two or three miles, and a church somewhere near, they must keep up their lessons at home."

On the shelf that Father had put up along the

[158]

wall, lay a letter addressed to Grandmother, back in Vermont. Each one of the family had written a part of it, but they had put all the pages together, for postage was high and they did not want her to have to pay too much when it reached her. Each one had ended with, "I would like to see you very much, and I hope sometime you can come out here to live with us."

"The next time I go to Lockport, I'll mail the letter," Father had said, "and I hope to find a letter there from her."

There was a big fire in the fireplace this cold morning. The pegs that Kanah had made had been used to put down a floor of basswood. Some of the rag carpet that Mother had brought from Vermont covered part of the floor. The oiled paper that had been put in the windows had now been replaced with panes of glass. The sled that Father had made for Kanah stood just outside the door.

In one corner was the big chest Father had made—not, to be sure, as beautiful as the lovely carved chest Mother had left in Vermont, but with plenty of room for the clothing and quilts. Mother herself was busy this morning dyeing some carpet rags.

"Hurry, Patty," said Kanah, crossly. "I want to get through my lessons, so I can go out to track animals."

"I am hurrying," said Patty, "but this example is a hard one."

"Oh, shucks! That one is as easy as rolling off a log," said Kanah.

"Maybe it is for you, but arithmetic is hard for me," said Patty. "I can beat you at grammar or geography any day, though."

Kanah couldn't deny this. He often wondered how Patty ever managed to remember so well where the rivers rose and how the countries were bounded.

All the time they were doing their lessons, they heard the sound of Father's axe, as it went *whack, whack, whack*. Every little while, they would hear a crash, as another tree went tumbling to the ground. Almost every day during all that cold winter, he went into the woods and chopped down trees, till the clearing had grown much larger than it was the fall before; and he had built a rail fence all around it.

Outside there was a huge pile of logs and cordwood which he and Kanah had dragged there to use in the fireplace. All day long smoke could be seen coming from the chimney.

At last the lessons were done. Kanah had put on his heavy coat, his fur cap, warm mittens and his heavy boots, and was starting out the door, when Patty said, "I want to go, too. I like to track animals as well as Kanah does."

Mother thought a moment. "Well, I suppose you do need some fun and fresh air and exercise," she said. "I had hoped you would be here to keep Mary Ann out of mischief while I dye these carpet rags, but I can manage."

In a few moments Patty was ready. As they were starting off, Mother said, "Patty is not to go out of sight of the house. If you go farther this morning, Kanah, she is to come back."

"All right," agreed Patty. She knew that, with the leaves off the trees, the cabin was in sight for a long distance.

They found rabbit tracks winding in and out all over the clearing and in the woods. They found squirrel tracks, fox tracks and tracks of other creatures that crossed and wound about through the snow. Kanah and Patty hoped that by following one of the trails, they would come to the home of the animal. Finally they followed a fox track far into the woods, halfway to Mr. Williams' house.

"Now you must go back, Patty," said Kanah. "You won't be able to see our house much longer."

"Oh, pshaw!" said Patty. But she knew she must do it, so she turned and went back alone.

Two hours later, when they were at dinner, Kanah came running back. By the look on his face as he dashed in at the door, they knew he had something exciting to tell.

"Did you know that Mr. Williams has sold out and moved away?" he shouted.

"No, we hadn't heard that," said Father, "although he told me a few weeks ago that he might go back to Massachusetts. Is their cabin empty?"

"No; somebody is living in it," Kanah replied. "And who do you think it is?"

"How could we guess?" asked Mother. "There are new folks moving in all the time."

"Is it anybody we know?" asked Father.

"Is it anybody from back home?" asked Mother.

"Is it anybody I know?" asked Patty.

"Yes, you all know them," said Kanah, who had now kept his secret so long that it seemed as though he would burst, if he tried to keep it much longer.

"Tell us," said Father.

"Tom Marvin and his wife and the baby," was Kanah's triumphant answer.

"Tom Marvin! Well, I want to know!" exclaimed Father. "I call that good luck. Some one we've known all his life."

"I thought he went to a place far east of here," said Mother.

"Yes, he did at first," said Kanah. "I don't

know just how he happened to move, but he found Mr. Williams' place was for sale, so he bought it."

"Well, well, that is a mighty fine piece of luck for us," said Father. "I'll go right over and make them welcome to our neck of the woods."

"I'll go, too," said Mother. "Won't it be good to see some of the Marvin family once more?"

"Kanah must stay here with Mary Ann and tend the fire," said Father.

There was soon a little procession going through the snowy woods—Father ahead to make a path, Patty next, trying to step in his tracks, and Mother following.

When they had come to the cabin and had exchanged happy greetings, and the first surprise was over, Tom Marvin said, "This is the best luck. We didn't know we were coming to live so near to you, though we did know you lived somewhere in this region."

"How did you happen to move out here?" asked Father. "Wasn't the land good in that other place?"

"Yes, that was good land. Our corn and other crops grew splendidly, but there was no place to sell them—no city near. We figured that with the new canal near here, there would be sure to be a city and a market for our crops."

"And you are right about it," said Father.

[163]

That was the beginning of many a trip through the woods for the two families.

During the rest of the snowy winter and all the following spring and summer and fall, Patty went frequently along the winding forest path to visit Melia and the baby. Then winter came again, bringing cold winds and deep snow.

CHAPTER XXII

FIRE

IF is a little word, but it means a great deal. If Melia Marvin had not been sick, then she could have helped put the fire out and Patty would not have had to do it all alone. If Mother had not taken cold walking through the slushy forest path the day before, then she would have been staying with Melia that day, so Patty would not have been there at all. If Tom Marvin had not had to go away on business that day, then he would have been at home and could have put the fire out himself. If Kanah had not had to go searching for the cow, then he would have been there to do it.

When all these things are true at once, then you do have a state of affairs and some one has to think quickly and act promptly and bravely. If a log house in the woods catches fire in winter and if some one doesn't act at once, there is little chance that it won't burn down; and if it does, the folks in it, sick or well, will be driven out into the snow and cold.

It happened that all these things were true one day in February, 1825. It was about a year since Tom Marvin had moved into the Williams house. Melia Marvin was recovering from pneumonia. She was over the worst, it is true, but the worst had been pretty bad. Mrs. Armstrong had gone there, through the watery wood path, every day for a week and had taken such good care of her that she was out of danger. Then what should happen but that Mrs. Armstrong herself should waken one morning feeling too ill to sit up.

"Who will take care of Melia to-day?" asked Mother, as she lay back on her pillow. "She must not be left alone while Tom is gone away, and she must stay in bed covered up warm."

"Let me go," begged Patty. "I'll take care of her if you'll tell me what to do."

"Could you?" said Mother. "Do you think you could manage to keep the baby out of mischief and give Melia her hot soup every three hours and keep the fire?"

"I'd like to try," said Patty.

"I'll tell you how we'll manage," said Father. "I'll stay here to take care of you and Mary Ann, while Patty goes there, but Kanah must go with her. He can look after the fire and bring the water and milk the cow and watch out for danger."

Very proud did Patty feel, to be put in charge of such important things, when she was "going on twelve."

"With the two of them, Kanah and Patty, everything will go all right," said Father.

It was very early in the morning when they got there, for Tom wanted to get a good start. He left as soon as they arrived, saying he would try to be back before dark.

All that day Patty was busy with trying to keep the baby quiet so Melia could sleep, with warming up the soup that Mother had made the day before, with keeping the house tidy.

"It is so good of you to come and do all these things for me," said Melia. "I don't know what we would have done without your mother; and now here you are to take her place."

Kanah kept a splendid fire, bringing in more wood every little while from the great pile stacked against the cabin. Toward night he went out to the shed to feed the cow and to milk her, but he found that she had got out of the yard into which she had been put that morning.

He looked around all over the clearing, and when he didn't see her, he called, "Co' Boss! Co' Boss!"

That call always brought her if she were within hearing, but this time no cow appeared.

He ran to the cabin door and called in to Patty, "The cow has got out. I must go and find her."

"Don't stay long," said Patty.

"Shucks, no," said Kanah. "But everything will be all right. I have made a big enough fire so you won't have to put any wood on while I am gone."

But the cow had wandered farther than he thought, and after half an hour he was not yet back. Melia had fallen asleep. The baby was playing on the floor, when Patty suddenly noticed smoke coming in little curls from the roof near the chimney. She looked up to see where it came from and there she saw some glowing red wood where the chimney joined the roof.

"Oh, dear! Oh, dear!" she said.

Quick as a flash she did what she had always been told to do. She took up the bucket always left near the chimney full of water and tried to throw it up to the fire. But she couldn't throw it far enough.

There was no more water in the house. Without stopping to put on a hood or a cloak, she ran outdoors into the raw cold air and filled the bucket partly full at a pool which the melting snow had made near by.

"It is lucky there has been a thaw, so I don't have to run clear to the well," she thought, as she dashed back into the house and grabbed a dipper and threw the water up against the burning timbers. She could make it reach with the dipper, but the tiny bit of water did little good.

Back and forth she went between the pool of water outside and the smoking wall inside, never taking time to put on warm wraps.

"Oh, if Kanah were only here," she thought.

Then Melia wakened. "Oh, what has happened?" she exclaimed.

Then, as she smelled the smoke and saw the burning wood, she tried to get up to help, but she fell back fainting on the bed.

"Stay right there and keep covered up," said Patty, remembering that Mother had said that on no account should Melia get chilled.

She took the baby up and placed her on the bed beside Melia. "You can help by keeping the baby here," she said, and she was off again like the wind.

Every time she ran outdoors to get more water, she called, "Kanah! Kanah! Too—whoo—oo—"

Then she decided that she might reach the fire better by pouring water on the outside, if she could only get it up there. So she dipped a half pail of water and climbed up on the wood piled

[169]

against the house. It was a terribly hard thing to do, with the bucket of water in one hand and the wood wet and slippery underneath, but she succeeded in getting there and throwing the water on the flame.

Over and over Patty scrambled down the pile of wood, went to the pool and dipped up half a bucket of water and climbed back up the cold slippery wood and tossed the water. Her dress was torn in several places, her hair was tangled, her face was covered with dirt and grime, a sliver had pierced one of her hands and they had both become so cold and numb that she could scarcely hold the bucket.

"I can't stop," she kept thinking. "I must put that fire out."

Finally she could see that the flame was dying down. Even then she did not let up, but kept going back and forth to the pool for water and lugging it up the woodpile and dashing it on the place where the flames had been.

It had become almost dark before Kanah, coming back with the cow, heard her call and saw the smoke around the cabin. He came running, and took the bucket and kept on till the last bit of glow had died out from the wood around the chimney.

Patty tried to get back into the house, but fell

[170]

in a heap just inside the door. There Kanah found her a little later.

It was an hour before Tom Marvin came home.

"Hello, folks!" he said, as he came in. "I have had a longer day than I expected, for the road was full of mud-holes and I thought at one time that I would not be able to get home to-night, but I—" Here he stopped, saying, "What is the matter?"

There was Patty, who usually looked so neat, with her dress torn and bedraggled, her hair still tangled and her face as white as the snow outside.

"Oh, Tom, what do you think Patty has done for us to-day?" said Melia. "She has saved our house from burning down."

Then, when Melia had told him how Patty had fought it all alone and how she had braved the fire and had tugged the heavy buckets of water, he came over and took Patty up in his strong arms and said, "My! But that was wonderful! How can I ever repay you for it and for taking such good care of my folks?"

"I don't want any pay," she said. "I didn't do it for pay."

As Tom put her down, he turned to Melia and said, "I always knew there was a dauntless spirit in this bit of a girl."

"Kanah helped, too," said Patty, loyally.

When he was thinking over all that happened that day, was it any wonder that there flashed into Kanah's mind the words that Patty had spoken last fall when he was working on the pegs? "You just wait. Sometime I'll s'prise you. You'll just see what I can do."

CHAPTER XXIII

THE NEWS

WINTER passed and spring came. Spring passed and summer came— the summer of 1825. It was late in July, the time of the ripening of berries in the woods.

Mother said at breakfast, "Kanah, do you know whether the berries are ripe on the far side of the clearing? If they are, and if you and Patty will pick some, I'll make some raspberry jam to-day."

"Yes, lots of them are ripe," said Kanah. "Big ones they are, too."

He and Patty took baskets and started for the berry bushes, Patty with her sunbonnet tied over her brown curls.

Father said to Kanah as they passed the corn-crib, "I am going to the gristmill to get some corn ground to-day and I am leaving you in charge. Can you see that everything is well looked after?"

"Yes," Kanah replied. "I'll do my best."

He and Patty went on and were soon busy picking the berries.

"Whew! These are nice big berries," said Kanah, as he picked a luscious red berry and put it into his mouth.

"And such a lot of them," said Patty, as she put one in her mouth. "Wouldn't it be nice if money grew on bushes?" she added.

"If money grew on bushes and you picked a lot of it, what would you do with it?" asked Kanah.

As quick as a flash Patty replied, "I'd hunt till I found my string of gold beads and then I'd buy it back."

"I didn't know you still cared about those beads, Patty," said Kanah. "I thought maybe you had forgotten them."

"Oh, no, I'll never forget them," said Patty. "You see, they were not just ordinary beads. They meant something."

"I know," said Kanah. "I thought you would be sorry you sold them."

"I'm not one bit sorry," declared Patty. "I'd do it again, if Mother were sick and didn't have a warm place to stay nor a bed to lie on. But if money did grow on bushes, and if I could pick a lot of it and buy them back, why—I'd like very much to have them once more."

"You'll never see them again," Kanah asserted. "You might as well forget them."

Their baskets were full before long and they went to the house.

"Just see all the berries we've picked," said Patty, setting her basket on the table.

"They are very large ones, too," said Mother. She tasted one. "And aren't they sweet?"

She made them into jam and put it away in earthen jars to eat next winter.

When Father came home from the gristmill, he said, "I have some news that will make you all glad."

"News? What is it?" asked Patty.

"Two bits of it," said Father. "For one thing, we have letters from back home. I stopped at the post office."

"From Grandmother?" asked Patty.

"From the Marvins?" asked Mother.

"From both," Father answered. "But let me tell the other news first, for it won't take so long as to read the letters."

"What is it?" asked Kanah eagerly.

"The Erie Canal is to be finished soon, probably within a month or two, and there is to be a big celebration up here at Lockport. When the last bit of work is done there at the locks, the whole canal will be finished and boats will begin to go through the locks, from Albany to Buffalo and back."

"Boats going through the locks!" said Kanah.

[175]

"I'd like to see that." He had been to Lockport a few times and had watched the men working on the locks.

"It doesn't seem as if a boat could ever go up that big hill," he said.

"Some of the best engineers of the country have been working on that problem," said Father. "It has been a big job, but it is nearly done. This canal is going to mean a great deal to us folks who live in this end of the State, and it will help business in other parts of the State, even down to the big City of New York. Governor De Witt Clinton will be at Lockport at this celebration. How many of you would like to go?"

"I would," said Patty.

"It would be nice to go somewhere and see folks," said Mother.

"I expect Lockport is going to be a big city," said Father. "It has grown like a mushroom the last five years. You know only a few log cabins were there five years ago; and now nearly three thousand persons live there. We'll go to the celebration."

"Now let's see the letters," said Patty. "Did Jane write to me?"

"See for yourself," Father replied.

He took from his pocket a letter written on a

[176]

big double sheet of paper and spread it out on the table where they all could see.

"They all wrote on this one sheet," said Father. "They probably thought it would cost us too much for postage if they each sent a separate letter, but they wrote so fine that they managed to get a lot of news in this one."

He read aloud Mrs. Marvin's part of the letter to Mother. After giving the news of the village, she ended, "We'll surely be glad to see you folks again."

"See us? What does she mean? Are they coming out here?" asked Mother.

"Mr. Marvin's letter explains it," said Father. "He says they have decided to move out here so as to be near Tom and his family. He is going to buy some land as near this place as possible."

"Oh, goody!" exclaimed Patty. "Won't it be grand to have Jane near by? When are they coming?"

"They hope to come this fall sometime," said Father.

"Well, that is good news," said Mother. "Our old neighbors near us again!"

"Let me have it, please, so I can read Jane's letter," said Patty.

Father handed her the big sheet of paper. Jane's letter contained news about the girls and boys Patty and Kanah knew. Then she said,

"Isn't it grand? We are going to move out where you are. I have missed you so much, Patty. And now we'll be neighbors again."

"That is the best news," said Patty. "We can't walk to school together as we used to, but maybe we three can all have our lessons together. Can't we, Mother?"

"Yes," said Mother. "I'll teach you part of the time and Mrs. Marvin may part of the time."

"And what is in the other letter?" asked Mother.

Father laid it on the table. It was a finely written letter of three pages. The fourth one was folded over for an envelope and sealed with sealing wax. The first two pages were taken up with news of the relatives. Then came this:

"You have all written to ask me to come out there to live. Well, I see my way clear now, and how I do want to see you. The Marvins have asked me to go with them. So when they come this fall, you may expect to see me.
Your loving Grandmother."

"Oh, goody! Goody!" exclaimed Patty.

"Goody!" echoed little Mary Ann.

"That is splendid news," said Father. "I surely have missed my mother, but it seems like a big journey for her. I'll build an addition to the cabin, so she can have a good room all to herself."

"You have another letter," said Patty.

"Yes; that is for Tom Marvin. It probably tells him the same news. You may take it right over there, Kanah."

Kanah took the letter and was off across the clearing and through the woods to Tom's cabin, as swift as a deer. The Armstrongs' clearing was so much bigger and Tom's clearing was so much bigger, that the path through the woods was much shorter than when they first came.

Tom came the next day to talk over the news.

"That is great," he said. "If Father lets me know beforehand where his land is, I'll have trees chopped down and the logs ready, so we can quickly build the cabin after they come."

"I'll help you build it," said Mr. Armstrong.

"I'll help," said Kanah.

"Who would ever have thought there could be so many exciting things going to happen?" said Patty.

She had grown a bit taller than when she came here, but otherwise she was the same. Kanah was a bit taller, too.

"I'll help chop the logs and notch them," he said.

He took his axe the next morning and lopped off the limbs from some trees Father had chopped down. Patty was so happy and excited that she went around singing *Yankee Doodle.*

CHAPTER XXIV

REUNION

T HE day of the big celebration had come at last—October 26, 1825. The Armstrong family, dressed in their best, had left home before light and had come to the village of Lockport in the same lumber wagon in which they made the journey from Vermont, only without the canvas top.

A few days before this, a letter had come from Mr. Marvin, saying they would start from Vermont about the middle of October.

"They will reach here about the tenth of November," Mother had said.

"It is too bad they cannot come in time for the Canal Celebration," said Patty.

She and Kanah had been looking forward to this day for weeks. Wasn't it the most important event that had ever occurred in this part of the State?

As they neared the center of the village, they all got out of the wagon and Father tied Buck and Brindle to a tree. Then they walked along the street, the crowd becoming thicker all the time, as they went toward the bank of the canal.

It seemed as if all the three thousand people of Lockport and all the settlers for miles around were already standing on the bank of the canal or making their way there.

A procession of the people who were to be the first to go through the locks was just starting down the hill to the foot of the locks, where some boats were waiting for them.

"I wish I could ride up on one of those boats,"
said Kanah.

"I wish I could, too," said Patty.

"Only officials connected with the building of
the canal or prominent citizens along the route

Lockport

of it will be allowed to do that to-day," said
Father. "Those first ones in the procession are
the Canal Commissioners and the engineers who
planned this difficult piece of work. A great

[183]

deal of rock had to be blasted out before the locks could be put in, you know; and it took brains to plan it."

They stood and watched the procession, as the bands played and the people cheered. After the men had filled the first boat, about two hundred ladies boarded the second boat. Three or four other boats filled with people floated on the water at the foot of the locks.

"Where is Governor De Witt Clinton? I want to see him," said Patty.

Father looked at a little sheet of paper in his hand—the program of the day.

"Oh, he isn't here yet. He is going to board a boat at Buffalo, twenty miles away, where the end of the canal is. He will be on the first one to come from Lake Erie into the canal."

"I want to see him, too," said Kanah.

"He'll be here this afternoon," said a man standing near by. "He is expected about four o'clock, on his way down the canal."

"Can't we wait till he comes?" asked Patty.

"Perhaps," said Mother. "But it will make us rather late home."

"I don't have to stick by the rest of you, do I?" said Kanah. "I want to go over where the cannon is."

"Go where you please, son," said Father. "You can find us by searching long enough."

It looked as though it might be a hard task to find any one, for the crowds kept milling about. All sorts of persons were gathering at this spot near the canal bank. There were people in plain clothes of homespun and people in broadcloth. There were workmen who had helped dig the canal. There were settlers with their whole families. There were boys and girls and babies. There were fashionable ladies in dresses of cassimere or of heavy silk and big bonnets trimmed with ribbons and feathers.

People had come all the way from Rochester and Syracuse and Albany and even from New York. They had come by stagecoach, on horseback and by packet boat, for the canal had been filled with water up to the foot of this big hill, some months before.

Patty stood with Mother watching the crowd and eagerly waiting for the boats to begin to go up through the locks, when her glance fell on a well-dressed man in whose face there was something familiar.

"I have seen him before," she thought. "Where could it have been?"

Then there flashed into her mind a certain scene which she had never forgotten.

"I believe he is the very man," she thought.

He was walking past and would soon be out of her sight if she didn't act quickly. Then, in a moment, he was out of sight beyond a group of men, but in another moment she saw him again making his way through the crowd. She plucked up courage and ran after him.

"Oh, sir, aren't you the man who bought my string of gold beads once upon a time in an inn on the Mohawk Turnpike?" she asked.

He was a tall man. He now looked down into Patty's earnest face a moment before he replied, "Yes, I did buy a string of gold beads from a girl about your age in an inn on the Mohawk Turnpike. But why are you away out here?"

"We came here to settle," she replied. "We are pioneers." As she said it, she realized that she was proud of it.

"Oh, sir, I want to buy them back," she continued, never stopping to think that she hadn't found any money growing on bushes and so had none with which to buy them.

"I am very sorry," he said, "but I haven't those beads any more. I sold them over a year ago to a peddler in Albany."

"And that is the last I shall ever see of them," thought Patty, as she went back to the place where Father and Mother were standing.

The people who were to ride on the boats were all on board, but the boats did not start. The crowd seemed to be waiting for something to happen.

[186]

"Why don't the boats start up through the locks?" asked Patty.

A man who was standing near and who seemed to know about the arrangements said, "They are not going to start till the signal comes from Buffalo."

"The signal?" said Mother. "What signal?"

"A cannon shot," said the man. "The Governor and his party are there and are going to board a boat called *The Seneca Chief,* which is to be the first one to come down the canal. Just as it slips into the canal, the cannon nearest it will be fired; a few miles down the canal there will be another cannon fired as soon as the first one is heard; and soon we will hear one and this cannon will be fired. And so the news is going to be sent all along the canal from one cannon to another as far as Albany and then down the Hudson to New York."

"That is interesting," said Father. "I wonder how long it will take for the news to reach New York."

They found out afterward that it took one hour and twenty minutes.

Meanwhile, at Buffalo, a procession of the Governor of the State and the Lieutenant-Governor and many other prominent persons marched down and boarded the boat called *The Seneca Chief.* It was a packet boat, beautifully

[187]

decorated with flags and bunting and drawn by four gray horses.

As ten o'clock came near, a hush fell over the crowd at Lockport, waiting for the sound of the cannon to bring the news that the boat was on its way. Just at ten, the sound came booming through the air. The gunners at Lockport immediately fired their cannon and the sound went reverberating over the forest and the hill.

The first boat began to move into the lowest lock. Then such a noise as burst forth! The cannon was discharged again and again. The bands played. The people cheered. Explosions of rock added to the din.

When the boat was in the lowest lock, a gate was closed behind it so the water that was pouring into the lock from above couldn't flow out.

The water kept getting higher, thus lifting the boat. When the water was even with that in the next lock above, the gate between the two was opened, so the boat could glide forward into the second lock. Again the gate was closed, the water poured in from above and raised the boat to the next higher lock. Thus it kept on until the boat had been taken through the five locks and had been lifted the sixty-three feet to the very top of the hill. The other boats followed, the one with the two hundred ladies coming next.

When the crowds saw that the boats had really gone up the hill through the locks, such a shout as went up from the throats of the people! Such a noise of cannon! Such a din of explosions! For weren't these locks the greatest thing of the kind that had been done in all America, and wasn't this canal going to be of the greatest benefit to both East and West, and wouldn't it be a great help in settling this new land?

The first two boats to go through the locks drew up side by side at the top; and there were speeches and a prayer of Thanksgiving. Then the four boats started on west to meet the Governor's boat a few miles away.

Patty could hear snatches of conversation around her. "A wonderful thing this canal is." "It will help us to get money for our crops, for they can now be shipped down to New York." "Settlers will come out here fast now." "Women and little children won't have to take that long trip in the covered wagons any more." "Those packet boats come in only four days."

Now that this part of the celebration was over, the crowd began to scatter. Mr. Armstrong stopped to talk with settlers from other parts of that section—from Niagara Falls way, from down toward the lake, from Lewiston and Royalton. Peddlers hawked their wares about. Kanah was now here, now there, seeing the cannon fired, going close to the locks, watching the band.

Patty stood with her father and mother, looking here and there among the crowds, wondering whether Tom and Melia Marvin had come. Suddenly at a little distance, she spied some one who looked so much like Grandmother that she gave a little start, thinking, "How queer it is that two persons could look so much alike!"

Then, in another moment, she had darted away from Mother and was running up to the little old lady, crying, "Why, Grandma Armstrong! How did you get here?"

"Why, Patty. And so you are here," Grandmother was saying. "We looked and looked for you folks and had made up our minds that you didn't come to-day."

Patty had been so intent on greeting Grandmother that she didn't notice some other people standing near, till a voice said, "Aren't you going to speak to a friend?"

"Why, Jane! Jane!" said Patty. "How did you come so quickly?"

Before Jane could answer, Mrs. Marvin stepped up, smiling. Tom Marvin was grinning to see Patty so surprised. Father and Mother hastened over. Everybody talked at once.

It turned out that when they had reached

Albany and had found out about the packet boats, Grandmother said she was coming on one. Then Mr. Marvin said that Jane and her mother had better come that way, too. They had been here two days.

"When we found we were coming by boat we didn't have time to send you word," they said. "We felt sure that you would all be here to-day, so we have been staying at the hotel."

"But aren't you dreadfully tired?" asked Mr. Armstrong of his mother.

"Not a bit," she said. "We had good berths to sleep in on that boat and chairs to sit in on top. No camping out in the rain for us."

"But you haven't told us where Mr. Marvin is," said Father.

"Oh, he is coming with one of the wagons," Mrs. Marvin replied. "A young man who is going to work for us is driving the other. They will be along in a week or two. I think they will come faster than you did, for they have horses instead of oxen."

"It just seems like a dream," said Patty.

"Shall we wait to see the Governor?" asked Father.

"Yes, of course," said Grandmother. "I would like to see the man who could put through such a big undertaking as this canal."

So they had some lunch and stayed till the

firing of cannon, about half past four, announced that the boats with the Governor and his party on board were in sight. Then again such a noise of cannon and of shouting!

People crowded close to the edge of the canal to get a glimpse of the famous man and to see the gorgeous boat on which he was traveling.

"Just see those two kegs," said Patty.

On the deck were two kegs with an eagle painted on each one of them. On them were also the words, "Water from Lake Erie."

"What are they for?" asked Jane.

"They are going to be taken to the Atlantic Ocean," said one of the men. "That water is going to be emptied into the sea, to symbolize the mingling of the waters of the Great Lakes and the ocean."

There was something of even greater interest to Kanah and the girls. One of the boats was called *Noah's Ark,* for on it were animals from this western land to be taken down to New York and shown to the people there. There was a bear on it. There were two deer, two eagles, some other birds and even some fish in a tank. Most interesting of all, there were two Indian boys.

By the time the Governor had made a speech and had left the boat for a banquet at the hotel, it was nearly sunset. The Armstrongs and the

Marvins started home, Jane riding in the Armstrong wagon, so as to be with Patty.

When they reached home it was long after dark.

"It certainly seems good to see you here," said Mr. Armstrong to his mother.

"And it is mighty good to be here with you folks," she replied.

Then Patty showed her the room they had built for her.

"You are to stay with us always," she said.

CHAPTER XXV

THE GIFTS

THE next day Mrs. Armstrong invited Mrs. Marvin and Tom and Melia to supper. After the meal was over, they were all gathered around the fireplace talking over old times and new.

"There will be a surprise for you when our wagons come," said Mrs. Marvin to Mrs. Armstrong. "I may as well tell you now. The furniture you had to leave behind is in one of them."

"My lovely carved chest? And the highboy and the chairs?" asked Mother. "Oh, how good of you to bring them!"

"We thought you would like them, and with the two wagons it could be managed," said Mrs. Marvin.

Mother's face lighted up with pleasure, for she had always missed those good pieces of furniture.

THE GIFTS

Jane and Patty sat at one side of the fireplace. Kanah, at the other side, was whittling a piece of wood. Grandmother was already knitting him a pair of warm mittens. The rest of them sat enjoying the firelight and the talk.

"Just as soon as Mr. Marvin gets here and decides where he wants his log house, we men will all turn in and build it," said Mr. Armstrong. "Tom and I and Kanah have made the logs ready."

"That is kind," said Mrs. Marvin. "And that reminds me, we have brought a present for Kanah."

"For me?" he asked, in surprise.

"Yes," she said, as she put her hand into her pocket and brought out a small package. "We heard away out in Vermont what you did last winter, when Tom's house was afire. Well, ever since then we have wanted to let you know how much we appreciate what you did. So when we passed through Albany we bought this for you."

"Shucks! I don't want anything for helping Tom's folks," protested Kanah.

"I know; but you'll take this from us, won't you?"

"Oh, a watch!" he exclaimed. "A repeating watch! Ain't that grand?"

For once Kanah forgot his grammar.

"Thank you very, very much," he said. "It is

just what I have been wanting—a watch. But I never expected to have a repeating watch."

Patty and Jane crowded around Kanah to see the watch and to hear it strike, but Patty's attention was called back in a few moments by Mrs. Marvin's voice saying to Grandmother, "You make the presentation to Patty."

"Seems as if it ought to be you," said Grandmother.

"No; you had a part in it," said Mrs. Marvin.

"Well, ever since I heard about what took place on the Mohawk Turnpike, I had wanted to get another string of beads for you, Patty," said Grandmother. "Then, when we learned about something that took place right here in these woods, when you worked so hard to keep Tom's cabin from burning down, Mrs. Marvin wanted to give you something for a remembrance, so we joined together."

"But I don't want any pay," said Patty.

"Of course not, but when we reached Albany and went into a jewelry store there, we found something that we thought might please you, so we bought it."

She handed a little box to Patty.

"Oh, a string of gold beads in place of the other ones! Aren't they pretty!" she exclaimed.

Jane's eyes were twinkling all this time, as she watched Patty's face.

"We thought they were pretty," said Mrs. Marvin, smiling.

"They are just like my other ones," said Patty, examining them. "Just exactly the same size, too. Thank you very, very much."

Then, as her eye fell on the clasp, she said, "Why! It is my old string of beads! Isn't it? Here are my initials made in just the same way. How did that jeweler happen to have them?"

"All we know is, that he said he bought them from a farmer's wife, who sold them to pay her passage on a packet boat to come west," Mrs. Marvin replied.

"Oh, I am so glad to have them again!" said Patty.

"If ever a girl deserved those beads, you surely do," said Jane. "First you won them by working patiently on your sampler. Now you have won them again by doing a brave deed, so now they are yours for good."

"I agree with you," said Father.

"Put them on," said Grandmother. "I want to see if they are as becoming to you out here in the wilderness as they were back in your nice home."

Patty slipped them on her neck and they gleamed in the firelight against the merino dress.

"The wild animals will stand and admire you,

instead of eating you up, if they meet you in the woods with those on," said Kanah.

When the guests had gone home, Patty went up to Grandmother and said, "I am so glad you have come to live with us. And I think it is wonderful the way my beads came back to me."

She took them off and placed them in the little leather trunk. A few years later, when the new house was built and Patty had a pretty room of her own, the trunk always stood at the head of her bed, and many a time she was asked to tell the story of

THE TREASURE IN THE LITTLE TRUNK

FINIS